BRAND: LOBO

Jason Brand was assigned to track down a renegade half-breed called Lobo, who was terrorising the territory and killing innocent people. Part white and part Apache, Lobo didn't belong to either society and had a grudge against the world. He was causing a deal of unrest and was wanted by both the whites and the Apaches. Brand realised that he had a hard task ahead of him and decided to seek the help of the Apache leader, Nante . . .

NEIL HUNTER

BRAND: LOBO

Complete and Unabridged

LINFORD
Leicester

First Linford Edition
published 1997

British Library CIP Data

Hunter, Neil
    Brand: Lobo.—Large print ed.—
Linford western library
1. Western stories
2. Large type books
I. Title
823.9′14 [F]

ISBN 0–7089–5139–2

Published by
F. A. Thorpe (Publishing) Ltd.
Anstey, Leicestershire
Set by Words & Graphics Ltd.
Anstey, Leicestershire
Printed and bound in Great Britain by
T. J. International Ltd., Padstow, Cornwall

This book is printed on acid-free paper

1

THE meeting had been set in a town called Rawdon.

It sat at the base of a high bluff. A sunbleached collection of buildings that had long ago ceased being anything but functional. The town did serve a purpose. There were a number of large cattle outfits in the outlying territory, and three hours from the town was the unimpressive outpost of Fort Kellerman. Rawdon existed as a supply base for the ranches, a weekend provider of entertainment for the cowhands and off-duty soldiers from the fort.

Colonel Alex Mundy, never a man to conceal his feelings, found Rawdon dirty and uncomfortable. It wasn't that he was unused to the conditions of frontier life. Thirty years in the Army left a man with few illusions. In his time

Mundy had experienced worse places than Rawdon, but he still objected to the town's indifference. Fort Kellerman wasn't one of the military's showcases but at least those in occupation tried to keep the post in a reasonable state of repair. As he sat on the porch outside Rawdon's only hotel, which some wit had named the Southwest Palace Hotel, he decided that it was an attitude of mind that made the difference. The Army instilled in its men the need for discipline. For order and upkeep. It was part of the military strategy, and it worked most of the time. Here in Rawdon there was no sense of pride. No sense of purpose. Rawdon lived for each day and spent each night adding up the profit.

Mundy stretched his long legs. He was hot and sticky in the restricting closeness of his uniform. He ran a finger round the tight collar of his jacket, glancing across the dusty street at the saloon facing him. His escort from Kellerman was in there.

A sergeant and two privates. Mundy wished he was with them. A glass of beer would have gone down very well. But that was impossible. He was a Colonel in the Army of the United States, and as such he could not allow himself the privilege of entering such a place. Alex Mundy was a stickler for protocol. He made hard rules for the men under his command and expected those rules to be obeyed to the letter. So he couldn't go breaking them himself — which right at this particular moment in time was a hell of a way to have to run an Army.

It hadn't always been so. In his day Mundy had been a hell raiser. He'd done his share of drinking and womanising along with the rest. But age and especially rank had forced these pleasures out of his life.

He stood up and paced to the edge of the boardwalk, facing along the street, narrowing his eyes against the glare of the sun. *God, it was damned hot*! The heat was all-enveloping, the air stifling. Heat waves shimmered out on the salt flats beyond Rawdon's east end. Mundy fished out his watch and glanced at it. Two minutes to noon. He wondered if Jason Brand was going to be late. It was almost three years since he'd seen Brand, but he doubted the man had changed his habits much. If that was true then Brand would be in Rawdon by noon.

Closing the watch Mundy put it away. When he raised his head again Brand was riding in. Mundy watched him trail along the street and up to the hotel. The horse Brand rode was streaked with dust, and so was the dark suit he was wearing. Brand reined in at the hitching post and dismounted. He tied the horse, turned and stepped up onto the porch, one big hand held out to greet Mundy.

"Been a long time, Jason."

"Too long," Brand said. He tapped the gold braid on Mundy's uniform, "Looks good on you, Alex."

Mundy smiled. "I was better off a

Major. Since they gave me these I spend most of my time behind a desk."

"You've earned it."

"From what I hear you've been earning a reputation yourself." Mundy led the way to the chairs that stood against the hotel front. "That was a rough deal you got when they threw you out of the US Marshal's office."

Brand flicked dust from the front of his jacket. "*Yeah*!" he responded, his tone indicating to Mundy that there was nothing else to be said.

"At least you're with a good outfit now. McCord speaks well of you."

Brand glanced at him. "You know McCord?"

"I've known Frank McCord for a long time. He's a good man."

"He's a mean son of a bitch," Brand said shortly.

"That too." Mundy smiled. "Any man who can get you to wear a halfway decent suit can't be all bad."

Brand ignored that remark. He

hooked a chair to him and sat down.

"Come on, Alex, I didn't ride all this way just to listen to you making funny jokes about the way I dress."

Mundy settled himself, staring out along the empty street while he collected his thoughts.

"What did McCord tell you?"

"That you've got a problem with a half-breed who figures he's going to wipe out all the whites *and* Apaches in the territory."

"That sums it up pretty well," Mundy agreed. "His name — his given name — is Matthew Henty. The Apaches named him *Lobo*. Because he's like a maverick wolf. They figure he's crazy and I don't think they're far off the mark. He's been running wild for the last twelve months. Killing anyone who crosses his path. Burning property. Butchering cattle and horses. Jason, he's run the Army ragged. He can move faster than we can. By the time a patrol picks up on one of his raids he's long gone. Has

6

himself a hide-out in the mountains somewhere. Even the Apache can't find him, and they want him as much as we do."

"McCord didn't say, so maybe you can tell me. What's his beef? Why is he so stirred up?"

Mundy shrugged. "*Quein sabe*? As far as anyone can figure he has a grudge against the world because he's a half-breed. Part white, part Apache. He doesn't belong to either society. He's a bitter man, all burned up with vengeance, and he's causing a lot of suffering. Jason, I don't give a damn about his problem. He isn't the only half-breed in the territory. Others manage to get along. What makes *him* so different? All I do know is he's killing too many innocent people along the way. He's making our job intolerable. His killings are causing a deal of unrest. Both sides are starting to blame the other, and we're in the middle trying to keep the peace. We can do without Lobo's interference. I

7

want him stopped, Jason, and you're the man to do it."

"You sound like McCord. Between the pair of you I'm going to end up convinced."

"You know this territory better than most."

"Sounds as if Lobo knows it too."

"I'll give you that," Mundy agreed.

Brand took a thin cigar from his jacket and lit it.

"McCord mentioned a lead."

"Lobo's half-sister is in the area. She's been trying to hire a guide to take her up into the mountains. Now she isn't letting on who she really is, or the reason why she she's here. Apparently she's posing as a woman looking for her husband. Something about him being on a geological survey for the government. She's calling herself Elizabeth Corey. That's half true. Her real name is Elizabeth Henty. She and Lobo had the same father, different mothers."

"And you figure she's looking for

Lobo?" Brand considered for a moment. "Any particular reason she should want to find him?"

Mundy shrugged. "Nothing definite. Their parents are all dead. Lobo is all the family she has. Maybe she wants him to give himself up."

"Not much of a future there," Brand said. "He comes in he'll hang."

"No question. Lobo has been offered amnesty three times. Last time they tried it Lobo sent the messenger back minus his hands and both eyes burned out."

"Sounds a nice feller."

"Jason, he needs to be stopped. For good. I don't give a damn how you do it. If you can get him in your sights long enough for a clear shot finish him."

"Where's the girl now?"

"Two days' ride from here. In Gallego. Still trying to hire a guide."

Brand knew Gallego. It was a flyblown town that straddled the border. A haven for any desperado riding the outlaw trail. Gallego owed no allegiance to any kind of law except the kind a man carried on his hip. If Elizabeth Henty was in Gallego looking for a guide, then she was getting desperate.

Mundy stood up. "I wish I could give you more help."

"Don't make it too easy, or McCord's going to figure I'm being paid for doing nothing."

They shook hands before Brand returned to his waiting horse.

"Don't make it another three years," Mundy said.

Brand raised a hand. "Look after yourself, Alex."

He left Rawdon as he had entered it. Unnoticed for the most part, and only Alex Mundy knew why he'd been there. Once clear of town he turned his horse south, picking up the trail for Gallego.

It felt good to be involved again. Not that he'd had much time for brooding since taking up McCord's offer. That had been over a month ago, and during that time Brand had found himself at the centre of an intensive round of instruction at McCord's headquarters outside Washington.

The place was a white painted horse ranch set amongst green trees and lush grassland. Behind the working facade of the ranch the real purpose of McCord's department was revealed. McCord had a small but dedicated staff and the most up to date organisation his budget allowed. Brand found himself being impressed with each passing day. McCord expected every man to master his own particular talents, and to that end Brand spent long hours on the firing range located in the basement beneath the main house. Here he was shown and given the chance to use the very latest in weaponry, from the smallest handgun to the most powerful rifles being manufactured. The instructor, a stocky, grey-haired man named Whitehead, watched Brand's technique and gave him a few discreet pointers. It was obvious that Whitehead knew his business and Brand took the man's advice. It later proved to be more than sound.

"And you can forget all that nonsense you hear about fast draw," Whitehead said one day. "I've seen enough to know it doesn't mean a thing. Concentrate on putting your shot where it matters. Most of the speed men are in it for the glory. I'm not saying being fast isn't important. Sure it is — but only up to a point. Hell, it doesn't help being fast if you can't hit anything when you get your gun out. The first bullet is the one that matters. Put that in the right place and your man will go down. Hit him off target and he'll likely stay on his feet long enough to put one in you." Whitehead stopped speaking suddenly, scowling at Brand. "What the hell am I telling you all this for? Damn little you need from me about handling a gun."

"When it comes to staying alive I'll listen," Brand had told him. He emptied the used casings from his

Colt and handed it to Whitehead. "Be obliged if you'd check it over for me."

Whitehead had returned the gun the following day. It had been thoroughly cleaned and oiled. The action was smooth and easy, the trigger pull feather light.

"See how she handles now. That pull is as light as it can be without she goes off every time you breath."

And then there had been Kito, a smiling, bland little man who had shown Brand a deadly form of unarmed combat from his native Japan. The first few sessions had left Brand badly bruised, and more than a little angry that this little man could render him helpless with a few swift moves. Kito, however, was a good teacher and Brand soon adjusted to the unfamiliar moves and actions. In the short time he was at the ranch he had many sessions with Kito, and by the time he left he had an insight into the Japanese way of fighting, becoming reasonably skilled in the use of a few throws and armlocks.

During his time at the ranch Brand never once met any of the other field operatives, as McCord called them.

"You won't," McCord told him in answer to Brand's inevitable question. "Operatives stay unknown to each other. It's a safeguard against possible threats to the security of the department. It's the way I've always run things and it works. We don't carry files on our operatives either. Once a man joins the department all the original paperwork we've built up is destroyed. In the unlikely event of anyone ever breaking in here — " McCord had smiled " — there wouldn't be a thing for them to find."

"All in the family," Brand had said.

"I have one or two people in the military who deal through me. People I trust. No one else."

Brand's grudging respect for McCord grew. The man was hard, sparing no one, least of all himself, but it was plain to see that he got results.

"I have an assignment for you," McCord said as he appeared beside Brand one morning on the firing range. "Get your gear together. Your train leaves in a couple of hours."

"Where to?"

"New Mexico. Home ground for you, Brand. A meeting has been set for you in a town called Rawdon. An old friend of yours will be there to fill you in. One of my friends, too. Army man. Name of Alex Mundy. It seems he's having a problem with a renegade half-breed called Lobo, and he's asked for our help."

2

BRAND rode into Gallego about mid morning. The dark suit had been exchanged for clothing more suited to his role as a guide. He hadn't shaved since leaving Rawdon and the dark stubble on his face added to his appearance. He felt comfortable now, in the worn shirt and faded pants, and he acknowledged that it was going to take time to get used to the formal dress McCord insisted on when his operatives were in Washington. Brand dropped his hand to the holstered Colt riding on his thigh. Once he had strapped on the gunbelt he had felt really secure. As he put his horse along the dusty, rutted strip that served as Gallego's main drag, he eased the hammerloop off, leaving the Colt clear if he needed it. Life was very cheap in a place like Gallego. He wasn't looking for trouble. On the other hand it paid to be cautious. The people who frequented Gallego were generally the lowest of the low. Men who would pick a fight just for the hell of it. They were in Gallego because there was nowhere else for them to go. It was the final resting place before the grave for a lot of them. They had nothing to lose, nothing to fear, so they were willing to take the ultimate risk.

He had smelled Gallego before he reached it. The stench of decay had filled his nostrils even across the flatland. Approaching the edge of town Brand had ridden by the deep pit where the town's waste was thrown. A skinny dog had raised its scabby head to stare at him, growling with menace. Its red eyes followed him until he was well by. Then it returned to its task of unearthing some foul piece of rotting meat.

Guiding his horse along the street, taking in the shambles that was Gallego, Brand wondered how such a place could exist. There was no plan to the place. The buildings appeared to have been constructed haphazardly. Simply constructed at a whim, with little concern as to the future. Perhaps because there never had been a true future for Gallego.

It had been a long time since Brand had been to Gallego. His previous visit had been during his US Marshal days. It had been a short visit, at night. He had been looking for a man and he had found him in one of the sleazy *cantinas*. The drinking houses seemed to be the mainstay of Gallego's economy. On the occasion of Brand's visit Gallego's noisy evening was shattered by a brief gunfight, during which time Brand's quarry had escaped through a rear door. Brand had followed and it had taken him another day of hard pursuit before he caught up with the fugitive. Now Brand was back in Gallego, seeing it in daylight, and wishing the darkness would fall. From what he recalled there was only one hotel in Gallego; if it could be termed an hotel. The place turned out to be a sunbleached wooden building with just a ground floor and one above. If Elizabeth Henty was stopping over in Gallego, then she would be staying here. Brand took his horse to the hitching rail, dismounted, looped the rein over the rail, and took his rifle with him.

The planks of the hotel porch creaked loudly as he walked over them. Brand went inside. The lobby was dim, the air warm and musty. At the desk Brand slapped the bell with the palm of his hand. After a minute a fat, wet-faced Mexican pushed his way through the beaded curtain that led to his quarters behind the desk. He was shoving the tail of his shirt into his pants. Before the curtain settled back in place Brand caught a quick glimpse of a low bed in the room beyond. On the bed was the naked form of a darkhaired Mexican girl. Her brown flesh glistened with sweat as she caught Brand's eye and flashed her white teeth.

"You want a room?" the fat Mexican asked.

Brand managed a smile. "Yeah. Hurry it up and you can get back to your friend before she loses interest."

The Mexican frowned for a moment. Then he leered at Brand. "That one never loses interest, *señor*. But I thank you for your concern."

"Talking of women," Brand said. "I heard there's an American lady looking for a guide. She staying here?"

The Mexican nodded. "*Si*. She is here in town. A very nice lady. She seeks her husband. He is lost in the San Andres somewhere. She wants a guide to take her there. But no one wants to go to that place. It is too dangerous. What good is money if a man is dead?"

"What's to be scared of?" Brand asked. "Most of the Apache have gone now."

The Mexican's eyes stared wide and round at him. "Have you not heard of Lobo? The crazy one?"

20

"The half-breed?" Brand shrugged with feigned indifference. "Hell, it's only a name. He's a man like the rest of us. But a bullet in him and he'll bleed like me or you."

"Not that one, *señor*. He is different. Not even the Army can catch him. He is evil. *El Diablo* himself." The Mexican paused from tucking in his shirt, leaning across the desk like some sweating conspirator. "I would not go into those mountains for 10,000 dollars. Not even for one as beautiful as *Señora* Corey."

"You got any idea where she is now?"

"A little while ago she went over to the *café*." He pointed to a flat-roofed adobe across the street.

"Hold on to this for me," Brand said, passing his rifle to the Mexican. "I were you I'd get back to your cousin. She's liable to grow old on you."

"No, *señor*, she will not get old. She is only seventeen. And she is not my cousin — she is my niece."

Brand took a slow walk across to the *café*. Pushing open the door he went inside. The first thing he noticed was the smell of the food. The odours of spiced meat and hot fat. The place hadn't seen a breath of fresh air since the day before the roof was put on. The *café* was around half-full — only one table interested Brand.

He didn't need to look twice to realise that the darkhaired young woman sitting at the table furthest away from him was Elizabeth Henty. He made a mental note to remember that for the moment she was Elizabeth Corey. As he crossed the room he saw she wasn't alone. A man was sitting at her table, while another stood at her elbow. From the expression on her face it was obvious she didn't want their attention. Brand tensed up. If he pushed his way in there could easily be trouble. On the other hand he needed to get to her before anyone else took the offer she was holding out.

He neared the table, and found he

could hear what was being said . . .

" . . . and it ain't likely your old man's still alive up there," the seated man was saying. "So why waste all that time lookin' for him? Sam and me, why we'd be tickled pink to have you come stay with us. Ain't been a woman like you round here for a coon's age. Right, Sam?"

The other man nodded. "He's right there, missy. And it's right what he says about you chasin' all over them mountains tryin' to find a feller who's most likely a pile of bones by now. Don't figure him much of a man leavin' a prime woman like you on her own. Real waste. Now Joe and me, we're alive, and ready to give you plenty of what you've been missing since your old man upped and left."

Elizabeth Henty's hand swept up off the table. She was holding a cup of coffee in the hand, and she threw it in Sam's face. He gave a sharp squeal, stumbling away from the table, pawing at his stinging flesh.

Joe kicked his chair back and rose to his feet.

"*Damn you, bitch!*" he yelled. His hand lashed across her face.

Brand reached him before he could hit her a second time. He caught Joe's arm and spun the man round to face him. Off balance Joe was unable to defend himself. Brand rammed a hard fist into the soft belly, and when Joe doubled over Brand clubbed him across the back of the neck. Joe was slammed face down onto the floor, moaning softly. As Brand turned away he caught a glimpse of a moving shape coming at him. He tried to pull aside but Sam's fist caught him across the jaw, knocking him back against the wall. Brand tasted blood in his mouth from a cut lip. Sam was coming in at him again. He had a thin-bladed knife in his right hand now. Brand recognised the killing rage in Sam's bright eyes, the gleam of saliva flecking his lips. Brand watched the knife, then Sam's eyes. He saw the flicker in the pupils as Sam made the mental decision to strike, and Brand was ready as the blade flashed in the light, slashing round in a deadly arc that was directed at his throat. Brand swayed to one side, grabbing for the wrist of the hand that held the knife. His fingers clamped on the wrist, his other hand gripping Sam's arm higher up. Almost before he realised what he was doing Brand had turned in towards Sam's body, pushing his shoulder against the man's chest. He had kept hold of Sam's wrist, twisting it and turning the arm over, then slipping his shoulder under the other's rigid limb. Then he straightened up, pulling down on the wrist. Sam let out a shrill scream as he felt his arm being bent against the joint. Brand gave him no chance to free himself. He slammed his right elbow into Sam's side with crippling force. A rib broke with a soft sound. The knife dropped from Sam's fingers. Brand kicked it aside. Then he turned on Sam, driving his fist into the man's face. Sam went backwards over the table, rolling heavily to the floor, blood spilling from his slack mouth.

Bending to pick up his fallen hat Brand made a mental note to tell Kito that all those punishing unarmed combat lessons were paying off.

He wiped blood from his lip as he crossed to where Elizabeth Henty stood. There was a livid red mark across the cheek where she had been hit. She had her eyes on Brand all the while. Looking at her he realised she was an attractive woman. He felt a warm stirring just staring at her and pushed the sensation aside. It still didn't stop him from looking.

He figured she was around twenty-five years old. Her thick, shining hair was very dark, as were her lustrous eyes, and she had an intense way of studying him that bordered on the unnerving. She had a wide, firm mouth, but the lips were full and pouted slightly. The body beneath the white shirt and dark skirt was strong and mature, yet still hinted at her youth.

"You all right?" he asked, conscious he'd been staring too long.

She nodded. "Yes. Thank you. I don't know what I would have done if . . . "

"Let's forget about that. We should get you out of this place. We can't talk here."

A dark eyebrow lifted. "Do we have things to talk about?"

"I reckon so. Story is you've been looking for a guide to take you into the San Andres. Truth tells you haven't found one. Now I need a job. I also know the mountains. By my reckoning I'd say we talk."

He led her out of the *café* and across to the hotel. The fat Mexican was leaning on the desk. He raised his head as they entered. Recognising Brand he handed over the rifle.

"That was quick," Brand observed, nodding towards the back room.

The Mexican shrugged. "I did not think you would be long. So I thought

I would wait until you came back, *señor*."

Brand took the room key the Mexican handed him.

"Now you can go back to her, *hombre*."

Brand trailed Elizabeth Henty up the narrow staircase. He checked the number scribbled on the greasy card tab tied to his key. He located the room and opened the door. Over his shoulder he sensed Elizabeth Henty waiting.

"My room or yours?" he asked.

A whisper of a smile touched her full lips. "I do hope no one heard that. We haven't even been properly introduced."

"The name's Brand, Mrs Corey. Now we have that out of the way can we talk business?"

"Are you always so impatient, Mr Brand?"

"No, ma'am. With certain things I take my time."

A faint flush of colour darkened her

cheeks. "You are no gentleman, Mr Brand."

"No, ma'am, but I'm the best guide you'll find in this territory. And I'm honest."

He held the door wide open for her. Elizabeth Henty swept into the room, her face angry.

"Shall I leave this open?" he asked, indicating the door,

She glared at him. "Don't be so ridiculous."

Brand closed the door. He checked the room out with a single glance. He had been in cleaner, more comfortable jail cells.

Elizabeth Henty sat down on the only chair, her hands laid in her lap. Though she tried to hide the fact she was studying him intently.

"Tell me if I have it right, ma'am," Brand said. "You need someone to lead you into the San Andres? To look for your missing husband?"

She nodded. "That's correct. He's been missing for two months. He had gone into the mountains to carry out a survey for the Government. It's his work. He belongs to the Geological Survey Department."

"Was he alone?"

Again she nodded. "Yes. George always works alone. It's his way."

Brand let her tell the story, only interrupting with some minor query. He had to admit she could spin a pretty good yarn. He was almost ready to believe she did have a husband up in the mountains.

"So why are you looking for him? Why doesn't Washington do something?"

She chewed at her lower lip, neat white teeth worrying the soft, pink flesh. "Oh, you have to understand the way the department works. They told me not to worry. Said George was always doing things like this on field trips. He goes off for weeks and no one knows where he is. Mr Brand, I don't care what Washington says. He wouldn't have gone off like this without letting me know." She stared at him, eyes wide open. "You see, we've only been married a few months. George promised he'd be back weeks ago. I just know something's happened."

Brand wondered for a moment if she did this sort of thing for a living. There was almost a touch of the professional about the way she told her tale. Especially down to the part about the deserted young wife. He pulled himself back to the moment.

"All right, Mrs Corey, what's the deal?"

She fumbled in her bag. "I have 500 dollars, Mr Brand. That's all. I've been advised that going into the San Andres mountains can be dangerous. I'm willing to pay the whole amount. Is it enough? For supplies as well?"

"There'll be enough, ma'am."

She was silent for a moment. "Why do you want to help me. Mr Brand?"

"Ma'am?"

"Everyone else has turned me down flat. They all say I'm foolish wanting to go up there. Yet you walk in and talk me into hiring you. Why?"

"I'm an easy touch where ladies in distress are concerned." Brand stroked his unshaven jaw. "And I'm flat broke, ma'am. I don't even have money to pay for this damn room."

Elizabeth Henty drew a wad of banknotes from her bag and handed them to Brand. "Now you have money," she said. She opened the door to leave. "By the way I am in room number 4."

Brand held up the money. "I *could* take this and ride out."

"I realise that, Mr Brand. I also know that you won't. Now when do we leave?"

"I'll arrange the supplies later. We'll get a good night's sleep and leave first thing in the morning."

3

BRAND purchased the supplies they would need. He walked his horse to the livery and made sure it was settled, fed and watered. Elizabeth's horse was there too. He looked it over. They had a long ride ahead of them and he wanted to be sure her mount would be up to it. He need not have worried. Among her other talents Elizabeth Henty possessed the ability to pick sound horseflesh.

He started back for the hotel. It was mid afternoon. The heat dropped from a cloudless sky. Gallego slumbered fitfully. The street was practically deserted. Brand felt the urge for a drink. He couldn't be sure about the quality of the whisky in Gallego — but he was about to find out.

There was a saloon a few doors down from the hotel. Brand made for it. He was halfway across the street when a lanky figure stepped out of the alley just ahead of him. The man held a rifle in his hands, and Brand recognised him. It was one of the pair from the *cafe* — the man called Joe. Brand could even see the dark bruise his punch had left on Joe's face.

"Let's see you walk away this time, you son of a bitch!" Joe said, his voice trembling with anger.

The rifle was already levelling on Brand, the muzzle abruptly jerking up towards Brand's face. It was Joe's mistake. The last one he ever made. He should have pulled the trigger the moment he had laid eyes on Brand, but his anger and his need to inform his intended victim what was going to happen, wasted precious seconds.

In any gunfight fleeting moments of time could mean the difference between life and death.

For the man called Joe his final seconds vanished in a flash of gunfire.

Brand simply dropped below the

muzzle of Joe's rifle, his right hand snatching his Colt from its holster. Crouching he thrust the gun forward and pulled the trigger. The heavy .45 calibre bullet hit Joe in the chest, shattering one of his upper ribs, the impact of the lead projectile driving fragmented bone into his heart and lungs. Knocked off his feet by the bullet Joe struck the ground on his back, a single wail of pain erupting from his mouth.

Before Joe had hit the ground Brand had turned, seeking the downed man's partner. His instinct told him that Sam would be around to back his partner, and if the pair were playing true to form Sam would be lurking somewhere behind Brand. Still in a crouch, his Colt cocked and ready, Brand's eyes scanned the shadowed boardwalk. He saw the furtive shape an instant before Sam opened fire. Brand saw the flicker of the muzzle flash, felt the burn of the bullet across his side. He snapped off a return shot and saw the figure stumble back, cursing wildly. Sam triggered again, his bullet gouging the earth behind Brand. A clatter of sound erupted as Sam collided with a stack of empty barrels on the boardwalk. Lurching away from the falling barrels Sam stepped off the boardwalk and used both hands to lift the massive Dragoon Colt he carried. Blood was already soaking through the front of his shirt. He took a faltering step in Brand's direction, the long barrel of the Dragoon wavering as he eared back the hammer. His finger jerked on the trigger at the same time Brand fired. Sam's bullet was way off target. The muzzle of the Dragoon flipped up under the recoil. And then Brand's bullet cored into Sam's skull. His head rocked back, a geyser of bright blood jetting from the entry hole. He did a slow turn, then pitched face down on the street, his limbs shuddering for a while.

Jason Brand stood in the street, ejecting spent cartridge cases from his

Colt. He reloaded the gun and ignored the gathering crowd. There were some hostile stares directed at him. It was as far as it went. Brand had shown what he was made of. There might have been friends of the dead men amongst the spectators, but none of them felt that friendship extended to bracing a man like Jason Brand.

It was generally accepted that Sam and Joe had walked into the fight knowing the risks. It was a lamentable fact that there was a need for personal vengeance within frontier society. A desire to settle arguments, or imagined insults, with a drawn gun. Brand hated the need for mindless violence it bred, but it was the way, and as long as he was involved with that society he was forced to live by its rules. He would have been the first to admit he had been tainted by the violence he rubbed shoulders with. There were times when he was as guilty as the rest. Resorting to the simple, direct expedient of instant justice. He wasn't proud of it — and his disgust often placed him in an intolerable position. In the end all his soul searching left him with the bleak acceptance of his fate. He knew he couldn't walk away from it. No matter how many times he tried.

Brand moved away from the crowd. Even the taste for drink had left him now. All he wanted was to return to his room and see to the aching wound in his side.

"*Hey, you!*" The voice rang out above the noise of the crowd.

Brand saw a large, red-haired man staring at him.

"You want something?"

The man cuffed his stained hat to the back of his head, "Damn right! Sam and Joe are dead. You goin' to leave 'em there?"

Brand holstered his Colt. "No concern of mine. They came hunting me. Trouble was they weren't up to it."

"Damn you, they need burying," the redhead said.

"They friends of yours?" Brand asked.

The redhead glared at him. "Damn right they were!"

"Then you bury them," Brand told him and walked away.

He tramped up to his room, slamming the door behind him. He tossed his hat across the room, unbuckled and removed his gunbelt. He dumped it on the bed. Stripping off his shirt he examined his side. The bullet had cut a ragged gouge over his ribs. The wound was sore and messy, but not serious. He crossed to the washstand and poured water into the chipped basin. As he put down the jug someone tapped on his door.

"Yeah?"

"It's me. Elizabeth Henty. May I come in?"

"Door's not locked," Brand said gruffly.

She stepped in, closing the door behind her. Her dark hair was loose, flowing about her shoulders. She was wearing a thin cotton wrapper, tied at the waist by a thin cord.

"I was going to take a rest. I went to the window to close the blind and I saw it all." She moistened her dry lips. "They would have killed you. Shot you without a chance."

"It's certain they weren't going to buy me a drink."

She glanced at the wound. "Can I help?"

He handed her a towel. Elizabeth moistened it in the basin. She began to clean the wound. Brand flinched as a surge of pain erupted.

"I'm sorry," Elizabeth whispered. Her face had paled.

"It's all right."

Brand found her closeness disturbing. He could smell her perfume. It was strong, heady. He could almost feel her body warmth as she leaned closer, intent on cleaning the wound. The cotton wrapper had loosened at the top, exposing the cleavage of her white breasts. It was impossible not to be aware of the way they moved as she breathed. He wondered if she was totally naked beneath the wrapper.

Elizabeth worked silently and efficiently. Once she had cleaned the wound she folded the towel into a pad and pressed it over the gash.

"Do you have anything I can use to bandage it?" she asked.

"In the pack over there," he said. "I bought some medical supplies."

Elizabeth located the bandage he'd purchased. She folded some into a fresh pad, then used a further length to wrap round his body and tie it in place.

"Grateful, ma'am."

Only then did she seem to become aware of his close scrutiny. For a brief time she held his gaze. Then she lowered her eyes, cheeks colouring warmly as she reached up and pulled the wrapper together to cover her body.

"You should rest," she said.

Brand glanced up from pulling a fresh shirt from his gear.

"Yes, ma'am," he said.

Her eyes flashed briefly, as if she had taken offence at his tone. "Will I see you later? For supper?"

"I'll knock."

Brand crossed to the window after she had gone. The bodies had already been moved from the street and the crowd had dispersed. In a few hours the talk would have waned and the shooting would have become just another incident. He leaned against the sill. It was a pity it had happened. It drew attention to him, and that was not needed. Brand sighed. He had been left with little choice in the matter. He regretted it having taken place at the start of his assignment. Not the most illustrious way to begin his new career. He slammed his hand against the window frame in frustration. Turning from the window he stretched out on the bed and stared up at the ceiling.

His mind was too full even to allow him to doze off. He couldn't get Elizabeth out of his thoughts. Or the way she had looked in that thin wrapper. Her supple body moving freely under the flimsy cotton. He sat up.

Damn her!

Why the hell did she have to be so attractive! He thought of the night ahead, and the fact that she would be sleeping in her room so close by. Restless and perspiring in the close heat. He cursed his over-active imagination.

It was going to be a long night.

Maybe he *should* go and have that drink. A whole damn bottle full of drinks.

4

BRAND didn't get drunk. After an early supper with Elizabeth he turned in and slept surprisingly well. They were up at dawn, and after a quick breakfast they saddled up and were riding out of Gallego as light flooded the eastern sky.

With the settlement shrinking behind them they cut off to the north. Later they would turn east, starting the long climb into the foothills of the San Andres range. For the present they trailed north. The land lay vaulted and scarred around them. It was arid and inhospitable. Dry and broken it was a place of emptiness, the rocks and cactus only adding to the vast sense of desolation. Dry watercourses crisscrossed the land like so many empty veins. There were countless gullies and crumbling, razorback ridges. To the

44

west, visible as they moved ever higher, was the muddy ribbon of water known as the Rio Grande, threading its way down into Texas and eventually the Gulf of Mexico.

They rode at a steady pace until noon. Brand found them a shaded place where they could rest. He made a small fire and put a pot of coffee on to boil. While it simmered he moved to a low ridge and took a long look around. The land appeared empty, but that meant very little. This was Apache country, and though there weren't so many of them around any longer they still posed a threat.

In another year the legendary Apache leaders would offer their surrender, realising that their tribes were close to extinction. For the present they continued to raid and kill. Brand knew the Apache well. He understood their ways. They were skilled and deadly fighters. They knew their land and they used every inch of the terrain to their advantage. It was said an Apache was not heard or seen until he decided it should be so, and by then it was too late to do anything about it. It was a notion closer to the truth than to fiction.

Lobo was foremost in Brand's thoughts. This was *his* land too. From what he knew of the half-breed, Lobo ranged far and wide. There appeared to be no boundary to the territory he covered. He had struck as far down as the Mexican border, equally as distant to the north. So as well as the Apache themselves, Brand was going to need to keep on the alert for Lobo. It would be ironic, he considered, if they were attacked by Lobo himself. He looked back to where Elizabeth sat beside the fire. She could be hurt in more ways than one during this trip.

He walked back to the fire. Elizabeth glanced up at his approach. They hadn't spoken much since leaving Gallego. Seeing him now she reached for tin mugs and lifted the pot off the fire.

"It smells good," she said.

Brand squatted on his heels across from her. She was dressed in a dark riding skirt, white blouse, and a short, soft leather jacket cut in the Mexican style. She had tied up her hair so she could wear a low-crowned hat.

He took the coffee she passed him.

"You mind it without sugar?" he asked.

She smiled. "I can manage."

They sat and drank, in silence. Brand felt Elizabeth's eyes on him, watching, searching.

"Are you a married man, Mr Brand?" she asked suddenly, her question direct.

It caught Brand off guard, dredging up half-forgotten memories.

"Had a wife once, ma'am. While back now. She's dead," he heard himself say. Leaning forward he picked up the pot and refilled his mug.

"I'm sorry," she said. "I didn't mean to pry. So — have you always been a guide?"

"No. I've scouted for the Army.

Wore a badge for a time. Hunted buffalo. Right now I'm a guide." He saw no reason to go any further. She was satisfying her curiosity; give her enough information and she would leave the subject alone.

"How long before we reach our destination?"

He smiled behind his mug at the abrupt change of questioning. Turning his body he pointed to the high peaks rising stark and bare into the sky to the east.

"That's where we're heading. Should reach those peaks in a couple of days. That's hard country up there. They call it the High Lonesome. Fits. We'll start to climb soon. If the weather holds we'll make good time. Then again we might run into the Apaches." He watched her closely as he added: "Or Lobo."

To her credit Elizabeth's expression didn't change. She held his gaze, swirling her coffee round in her mug.

"Oh, yes, I've heard about him. I

believe that's why no one would bring me up here. They do say he's worse than the Apache. Everyone seems afraid of him. Are you?"

Brand tossed out the dregs in the bottom of his mug.

"I get scared. Man has a right to up here. On the other hand you can't spend your life hiding from shadows."

He stood up and crossed to check the horses, pulling in the cinches. Elizabeth cleared away the utensils and smothered the fire.

★ ★ ★

They rode on through the afternoon. With the sun beginning to slide below the western horizon Brand took off to the east, the horses starting to pick their way up the first slopes of the San Andres. They kept moving until darkness forced them to stop. Brand found them a good place to make camp. There was a small group of rock pans holding water. *Tinajas*, the

Mexicans called them. Brand fixed a small cookfire, then moved to unsaddle and settle the horses while Elizabeth took over cooking a meal. By the time he returned from feeding and watering the animals, tethering them close to one of the pans she had salt bacon and beans in the pan. The smell of frying meat made Brand realise just how hungry he was.

"Should we be doing this?" she asked. "I mean isn't the cooking smell going to carry?"

Brand filled his plate. "If you're worrying about Apaches, don't. If they're around they'll find us whether we want them to or not. They'll know we're here already. Hiding fires and damping down cooking smells isn't going to make us invisible. Showing we're not going to be frightened off is a display of strength. They understand that. There's a lot of damn nonsense talked about the Apache. He's a whole lot smarter than people give him credit for."

"You talk as if you respect the Indian."

Brand's gaze turned towards her in the deepening gloom. "No reason why not. I've fought the Apache. Doesn't mean I can't respect them as fighters — and men." As soon as he had spoken Brand felt foolish; he was not used to expressing himself so readily; there was something about Elizabeth that brought words easily to his lips.

They finished their meal and after clearing up Brand extinguished the fire. Then they turned in. There was a good moon, layering the rocky terrain with cold, silvery light. Brand lay in his blankets, sleep eluding him for some reason. He could hear Elizabeth moving about restlessly herself. She seemed to be having difficulty settling down. He understood her state of mind. This trip would be hard on her. She would be wondering how her half-brother might receive her. Brand admired her for what she was doing. Unwittingly she was burdening herself with a great

51

responsibility. Lobo had proved himself to be a heartless, brutal killer, so twisted by his twilight existence that he hated both sides — white and red. If Elizabeth was expecting him to meekly lay down his weapons and surrender, then she was in for a big shock. Brand never had believed in miracles. It may have been his profession that had turned him sour. Yet he could understand the deep-rooted hatred that could develop in a man's mind. The appearance of a long lost sister was no guaranteed cure.

Brand considered, briefly, whether he should feel some guilt for the way he was using Elizabeth. He brushed the notion aside quickly. He was here to carry out the job he had been trained for. Feeling sorry for someone else could get him killed. It didn't do to get too close. Elizabeth Henty was here by her own choosing, and damned if she wasn't using him in her own way.

No — he had no right feeling guilty. His job was to get to Lobo and stop him. The way he achieved that goal didn't matter. Lobo was killing a lot of people. Disturbing the balance of peace in the area. He had to be stopped. And if he was forced to use Elizabeth to get to the breed then so be it.

He drifted into sleep eventually. When he opened his eyes again it was dawn, the light breaking with a chill over the peaks toward the east. Brand rolled out of his blankets. At one of the *tinajas* he splashed water on his face. The water was icy and made him wince, but it woke him fully.

He rekindled the fire and got breakfast on the go. The sliced bacon in the pan was close to being ready when Elizabeth sat up, stroking hair away from her face.

"Good morning, Mr Brand," she said, smiling.

As she walked to the water pans Brand noticed she kept staring at the distant peaks. It was as if she was looking for something — even though the peaks were too far distant to yield anything. He watched her rinse her face. She was still eyeing the far distant mountains on her way back, and he could tell she was scared by the thoughts of what she might find once she got up there.

"Hungry?" he asked.

She nodded absently. She sat staring into the flames of the fire. When he handed her food across she took it and ate, and there could have been anything on the plate. Her mind had wandered again, travelling far ahead of her physical body.

"We'll move on as soon as we clear things away," Brand told her.

Half an hour later they were ready. The horses stood impatiently by while the gear was tied behind their saddles.

Brand led off, taking them along the crest of a ridge that wound an easterly course. From here the way would become progressively steeper as they pushed up into the mountains. Travel would be slow. The high slopes gave way to stretches of broken, brush-choked terrain. Deep ravines, crumbling talus ledges and places where tumbled rock formed impregnable barriers. It was sun scorched, bitter country. Pale dust rose from under the hooves of the horses, leaving an acrid, stinging taste in their mouths. And still high above them towered the silent, bleached peaks, stark against the cloudless sky. Up there were the vast, silent canyons. Empty, lifeless places of towering cliffs and bottomless chasms. It was a place unchanged by the passing years. Man had put his foot upon the land, and when he had gone nothing would have changed. The mountains remained. They would always remain. Man made a shadow that lasted but a few fleeting seconds. The mountains were eternal . . .

5

BY mid morning the heat was intense. Sweat poured from them. The horses laboured wearily across a flat, wide-open stretch of bleached rock, hooves ringing dully on the flinty surface. They were heading for a soaring rockface that swept into the sky. It lay directly ahead of them. There was a way through that Brand knew of. A narrow canyon that drove deep into the heart of the solid mass of rock. From there they would be able to follow a near-invisible trail that would take them to the next bank of slopes, and follow along to the higher reaches of the mountains.

Brand reined in, easing in his saddle to check on Elizabeth. She caught his glance and smiled weakly, then realised his attention had already drifted from her to something that had grabbed him urgently.

"*Get down!*" he snapped harshly, his right hand snatching the Winchester rifle from the scabbard at his saddle.

Elizabeth didn't question his command. She threw herself from her saddle, stumbling as she landed. Brand was already off his horse, reaching out to take hold of her wrist and drag her to him. He pushed her roughly towards a shallow dip in the ground. As she landed Elizabeth heard the sudden, flat sound of a rifle shot. Moments later the bullet struck hard rock and whined off into the air. She realised how close it had been when she felt the patter of stone chips against her boots.

"*Here!*" Brand dropped down beside her, pushing her own rifle into her trembling hands. When she stared at him, not understanding, he said: "Apache."

He didn't waste time on more talk. There was enough to keep him busy. He had seen three of them, and that many seasoned Apache warriors were enough for any man.

They were somewhere in the scattering of rocks on the far side of open space separating them. Brand studied the lay of the land before him. The only consolation was that the Apaches had to cross the same open space if they wanted to reach him. They couldn't come in from Brand's rear. A few yards back a sheer rockface rose three-hundred feet into the air, but it was little comfort knowing that.

Brand glanced to where the horses stood. They had moved yards away, startled by the gunshot, but they had settled now. He didn't expect the Apaches to kill the animals. Horses were prized by the Apache. Never more than at this time when the Apache was fighting for his collective life. A captured horse would be a welcome prize. Something to brag about and something that could be usefully used on raids. It enabled the fighting warriors to move faster, to strike deeper and to get away safely.

"It might seem a silly question, Mr Brand, but what do we do now?"

Brand turned to look at her. Her face was a little pale. Apart from that she seemed calm enough. At least she wasn't the kind of female liable to faint dead away at any sign of trouble.

"Before I do anything I want to know just how many of them there are."

Out of the corner of his eye he sensed movement across the clearing. Turning in that direction he saw a lean brown figure dart from cover and make for a wide, squat boulder midway across the clearing. Brand pulled the Winchester round, snapping off a shot that laid a bullet into the ground inches from the Apache's flashing feet. The Apache threw himself forward, rolling easily and slid out of sight behind the boulder before Brand could jack a second round into the Winchester's breech.

"*Damn!*" he said forcibly.

"Another!" Elizabeth's warning was firm, insistent, and she was levelling her own rifle even as she spoke.

Before she could fire a thunderous crash echoed among the rocks. The Apache who had just shown himself was picked up and hurled forward as if struck by some huge, invisible hand. The brown figure crashed face down on the ground, limbs flopping loosely. The lifeless body skidded some yards before coming to rest on its back. There was a large, ugly wound, pulsing with blood and gore, in the naked chest.

Brand pulled his gaze from the dead Apache when he spotted movement by the squat boulder. The Apache he had shot at and missed showed himself. But not facing Brand. The Apache had turned and was aiming his rifle into the high rocks above his original position. Brand took the offered target, putting a single shot through the Apache's head that pitched him face down on the ground.

The surviving Apache began to place return fire into the high rocks, seeking the hidden gunman. His unsuccessful attempt was highlighted when the concealed gun boomed once more. There was a short yell of agony from the Apache, then silence.

Brand remained where he was, gesturing for Elizabeth to do the same. He scanned the high rocks above the Apaches' former position. He wasn't going to move until he knew exactly what was going on. He wanted to be sure that whoever had shot the Apaches was friendly. He had recognised the sound of the hidden gunman's weapon. It was a Sharps. The *Big 50* as it was widely known. A rifle designed primarily for the killing of buffalo, it delivered a huge bullet with terrible force. It was a sure man stopper.

He caught sight of a figure moving down out of the rocks. Brand watched as the man, leading a big chestnut, worked his way down through the tumbled rocks until he was on level ground. As the man got closer Brand was able to make out the heavy shape of the Sharps he carried.

Beside him he heard Elizabeth give a quick, indrawn breath. *She knew the man*!

"Friend of yours?" he asked.

"No. But I do know who he is. Or what he calls himself. Preacher Jude. He was in Gallego before you arrived. He came to me and offered his services. As my spiritual comforter."

"Your what?" Brand asked, turning to look her in the eye.

Elizabeth gave an apologetic smile. "Don't ask me to explain. I didn't waste any time trying to find out myself. To be honest, Mr Brand, I found him strange."

Brand turned back to watch Preacher Jude's final approach. The Sharps was cradled in the crook of his arm now, some concession to the suggestion that he was coming in peace. Jude was dressed in black from head to foot. The suit, with its long coat, was wrinkled and stained with dust. The pants were stuffed into the tops of scuffed, run-over boots. He even wore a black shirt and string tie. Jude's hat was flat crowned, with a wide brim. Up close Jude was a big man. Both tall and broad, his shoulders bulging under the taut cloth of his jacket. Brand did notice he was starting to run to fat around the waist. His thick hair was black and so was the heavy beard covering the lower half of his face. The eyes that peered out on the world were cold and flint hard.

Jude stood a few yards off. The empty eyes moved to Elizabeth as she climbed to her feet, held on her for a moment, then returned to Brand.

"Brother, I can see you are a man who doesn't trust easy." Jude's voice was rich and deep. The kind of voice that would have sounded good coming from a pulpit every Sunday in church.

"It's why I've stayed alive so long," Brand said.

Jude smiled, showing his large teeth. There was something in the way he smiled so easily that didn't settle too well with Brand. He was wary of the man and Jude's having turned up at such a convenient moment. Was there more to Jude's presence than just being a good samaritan? Brand wanted to know just how long Jude had been around. And why. They were questions only Jude himself would answer by his future actions.

Jude had already switched his attention to Elizabeth.

"I see you have found your guide, sister," he said. He made no attempt to conceal the way his gaze roved freely over her body.

"And you, Mr Jude, seem to be offering more than spiritual comfort," Elizabeth answered dryly.

He laughed, the sound booming out amongst the rocks. He touched the barrel of the massive Sharps. "We live among savages in a sinful world, sister. My way is the way of The Lord, and I do my best to follow his word. Those who sin must perish. I am but a tool of The Almighty, striking down those who walk the path of evil."

64

"I thought the Bible also said to forgive those who sin against you?"

"We each find our own meaning in the words, sister."

"Before we break into the psalms," Brand said, "I'd like to move on."

He turned and went after the horses, bringing them back to where Elizabeth stood. She mounted up without another word to Jude.

"Brother, I would ride with you a distance," Jude said.

Brand jammed his rifle in the scabbard, turning to face Preacher Jude. "We've a long way to go, Jude, and I don't intend wasting time. I'm grateful for what you did, but I reckon I can manage."

"There is a hardness in you, brother. My thoughts are for the woman. Two guns would be better than one." Jude indicated the dead Apaches. "Those bucks are from Nante's band. He finds out they're dead he's going to want a reckoning."

"Nante? He's around here?" Brand

asked as he eased into the saddle.

Jude nodded. "Surely so."

"Then we'll take our chances," Brand said. He saw the momentary gleam of anger that flickered in Jude's pale eyes.

"Thou art a stubborn man," Jude said tightly. "But I'll not force myself on you. Go on your way and may The Lord watch over you. I shall pray for you."

"Don't waste your time on my part," Brand said, and led out, with Elizabeth following close. He could feel Jude's eyes on him as they rode deeper into the canyon. He felt certain it would not be the last they saw of Preacher Jude. He was as certain of that as he was of the fact that if he could find the Apache called Nante, then he and Elizabeth would have safe passage throughout the San Andres. Safe from the Apaches that was. Somehow he didn't think it would extend to include Preacher Jude.

6

BY late afternoon they had cleared the canyon and were already on the high slopes, where the earlier rocky landscape was now relieved by pinon and juniper. The air was crystal clear and they could see for miles. In all that vast spread of mountain terrain nothing moved. They might have been the last people alive in the world, had it not been for the fact they were far from being alone. Brand knew they were being watched. Even though he had not seen anyone himself, he knew that hostile eyes were following them every step of the way. That they had not been attacked again was a good sign. It told Brand that Nante knew he was here, and the old Apache was biding his time. He would show himself when he was ready, choosing the moment to suit himself.

Brand made camp early. He noticed the questioning look in Elizabeth's eyes when he called a halt. It was still a good hour from sunset. She must have realised he had a reason, but wasn't prepared to tell her why, so she remained silent.

He had stopped near a small pool fed from a small spring. There was grass for the horses and trees for shelter. Brand built a small cookfire near a jutting overhang, noticing the sign around the area that told him the Apaches used this as a camp themselves. He filled the coffee pot and put it on to boil.

"Do you want to eat?" Elizabeth asked.

Brand nodded. She busied herself beside the pool preparing food. Brand went to the fire and sat back waiting for Nante to come.

When he did show Brand almost missed him. The old Apache stepped out from a shadowed stand of juniper and walked straight into the camp. Nante was easily sixty years old, yet he moved with a light step that would have been the envy of a young buck. His black, bright eyes were alert and quick. The brown, lined face was age old, yet there was something in the expression that told of Nante's will to survive. Old he might have been, but out of those long years had come much learning. The mounting decades had not dulled his senses.

Brand stayed where he was as Nante approached. As the Apache neared the fire Brand indicated he sit. As the old warrior squatted across from him Brand filled a mug with hot coffee and passed it to him. Nante took the mug, sniffing the coffee. A flicker of a smile creased his brown face.

"When we last spoke you gave me coffee," Nante reminded him, then drank deeply.

"I remember."

"That was a long time ago, Brand."

"Much has happened since then."

Nante held out the mug and Brand refilled it. "Then you rode for the

69

Army. Now you ride with a woman."
Nante glanced across at Elizabeth. She
was busy with the food. "She is your
woman, Brand?"

"No."

"But still you will take her to your
blanket?" Nante was showing his teeth
in a knowing smile.

"Maybe."

"You will take her," the Apache
decided. He emptied his mug. "Why
are you here, Brand?"

"I have come looking for Lobo."

Nante considered for a moment. "To
kill him?"

"If I have to."

"Who sends you to do this thing?"

"The people I work for in Washington.
And the Army."

"Do they expect you to capture
him?"

"They have left it to me to decide
what to do."

"Then kill him, Brand, or he will kill
you. Hear my words. There is no profit
talking to a mad dog."

"As always, Nante, you speak with wisdom."

Nante made an angry gesture. "Lobo! That one is bad, Brand. Evil spirits entered his body at birth and turned him against both races. Yet his mother, Tensi, was a good woman. His father, though a white, was a man of courage and honour. Yet Lobo hates us all. With every breath he hates. Because he walks between two worlds he is bitter, and his bitterness has poisoned him."

"Your people cannot find him?" Brand asked.

"In the old days we would have. We are too few now, Brand. Our time is short and we will have to surrender soon, or we will all be dead. Even now there is talk that Mangas, Cochise, even Geronimo, are thinking this way." Nante sighed, and for a fleeting moment he looked his years. "We are fighting to stay alive, Brand. A war we cannot win. Lobo is a crazy wolf at our heels, and we dare not weaken ourselves by sending warriors to search for him."

"Today three of your warriors died. If I had known you were here it might not have happened."

"I learned of your presence too late," Nante said. He looked through the flames of the fire at Brand. "You will not be harmed by The People. Nor the woman."

"Nante, she is Lobo's sister. She will lead me to him."

"Take care, Brand. Lobo is as deadly as the snake. Corner him and he will fight with the cunning of a wolf. Do not trust him."

"And what will you do, Nante, my friend?"

"We go south. To Mexico. There we can rest. Talk of the future." Nante stood up. "I wish you good hunting, Brand."

"And you, Nante."

The Apache turned and left the camp as swiftly as he had arrived. He slipped into the shadows of the trees and was gone within a heartbeat. Brand stared after him. He felt a deep regret when he recalled Nante's words. Soon there would be little left of the Apache nation. If their pride prevented them from surrendering and they fought on, they would finally be wiped out, and as far as Brand was concerned that would be a damned shame.

"You know him?"

Brand glanced up and saw Elizabeth was standing beside him.

"Yeah, Nante and me, we've been fighting each other for years."

"You didn't act like enemies."

He smiled. "We've reached an understanding."

"What were you talking about?" she asked, kneeling by the fire to cook the food she had been preparing. He sensed the underlying suspicion in her voice.

"I asked him if he'd seen a white man in the area. He said we are the first whites to come up here for months. You sure this is the territory your husband covered?"

Elizabeth's face darkened with annoyance. "Yes, Mr Brand, I am!"

She bent over the food and stayed silent.

Brand helped himself to more coffee. He studied the curve of her back as she concentrated on cooking their meal. She was getting touchy. He could expect more of that. The closer they got to Lobo the jumpier she was liable to become. She must have realised that whoever brought her into the mountains was going to ask questions about her make-believe husband. There would also come the time when all the pretence had to stop. Sooner or later she was going to have to reveal just why she was up here. What then? As long as Brand could locate Lobo's hideout, he wasn't going to worry too much about that moment. Even so he realised he was going to need to be careful. If Elizabeth got wind he knew who she was, and why he was with her, he might never get anywhere near Lobo.

They ate a silent meal that night.

Elizabeth had withdrawn into herself. She would only speak out of necessity, then only using words sparingly. The moment they had finished the meal and cleaned up, she went directly to her blanket and lay down. Brand took a turn around the campsite, checked the horses, then turned in himself.

He lay in his blanket, his mind refusing to relax. He found he was thinking about the man calling himself Preacher Jude. There was more to Jude than simply a fancy for Elizabeth. Did he know who she really was? If he did there could be an easy explanation for Jude's presence. There were a number of rewards out for Lobo and they totalled up to a tidy sum. New Mexico Territory itself was offering 10,000 dollars. A large cattle-combine had put in 8,000 and a group of civic-minded businessmen had added 5,000. A southwest stageline, that had suffered greatly at Lobo's hand through burned-out way stations, to stock being run off or slaughtered and employees killed, had put in another 7,000. Though the totals varied there was full agreement on one point. The money would be paid on production of Lobo — dead or alive. Preferably dead! Maybe the money was at the back of Preacher Jude's concern over Elizabeth. The reason he was wandering around the San Andres. Brand had no proof — but he always went with his gut feeling. It wasn't going to do any harm to keep a watch out for Preacher Jude. One thing he was sure of — Brand was going to see Jude again — and that time wasn't far off.

He pulled his blanket over him. He found himself looking across to where Elizabeth lay. Damned if Nante hadn't been right. He did want her. That was something else he was going to have to be patient about. Brand turned the other way, pushing the thoughts of Elizabeth to the dark recesses of his mind.

He lay for a time listening to the soft moan of the wind playing around the high peaks. Was Lobo up there listening to those very same winds? And Jude somewhere else on the mountain slopes? Matters were building to a head. And he was right in the centre of it all. Which he wasn't surprised at in the slightest. He had the knack of walking into trouble. Did it without conscious thought. Fate had a perverse way of complicating the simplest of matters, as if a man didn't have enough problems to handle without more being thrown into the pot.

He drifted off into a restless sleep, waking early. The sky was grey and overcast. The air held a damp chill and Brand had a feeling there was a storm due. He rolled out of his blanket. The fire was out. On his feet he glanced to where Elizabeth had laid her blanket. It was gone. So was her gear. He looked to where he had tethered the horses. His animal stood on its own. Elizabeth's horse was gone.

Damn fool woman!

His anger rose unchecked. He snatched

up his saddle and crossed to his waiting horse. He cursed himself for not paying her closer attention last night. She had acted odd from the moment Nante had shown himself. He had not expected her to do a damn fool thing like taking off on her own. He completed saddling up, gathered and stowed his gear, then hauled himself on board.

Elizabeth either didn't realise the danger she might be putting herself in, or didn't care. The reasons were unimportant. Placing herself in jeopardy could get her killed.

He had to find her.

Get to her before it was too late.

7

AS full light broke over the jagged eastern peaks dark, rolling clouds swept in, bringing the threat of rain even closer. A gathering wind rattled through the junipers clinging to the steep slopes. Far to the north thunder rumbled heavily. Within the hour the first rain fell, and within minutes it had increased to a savage downpour. It drove down out of the heights, sweeping across the exposed slopes in glistening sheets. Every stream, every trickle of water was suddenly burdened by the extra volume of water. It coursed its way down the mountain slopes, tumbling and foaming as each small stream fed the next, growing larger and heavier. The streams burst their banks as they roared and tumbled to the flatlands below, where eventually they would empty themselves in the Rio Grande. Storms were infrequent in this part of the country — but when they occurred their fury and intensity was extreme.

The full force of the storm caught Elizabeth Henty on an open slope. Bending in the saddle she forced her horse on, shielding her face against the driving rain, her body chilled by the cold wind that accompanied the downpour. She admitted she had been foolish to walk out on Jason Brand. He would have seen the storm coming and would have been prepared. With his knowledge of the mountains they would have been able to find cover before the storm struck. She had made her choice, though, and now she was going to have to face matters on her own.

She felt the horse stumble. Elizabeth hauled in on the reins, pulling the animal's head up. The horse refused to go any further. Sliding out of the saddle Elizabeth struggled to loosen her waterproof slicker from behind the saddle. Even when she had it free she had to fight against the tearing wind to pull it on. Pulling on the reins and talking to her frightened horse she finally got it to walk on, stumbling and slipping herself as she struggled up the waterbound slopes, the reins cutting into her fingers. Checking her bearing she saw that the peaks still lay ahead of her — and she knew that meant she was travelling to the east.

Narrowing her eyes Elizabeth squinted at the harsh outline of the dark peaks. She experienced a feeling of foreboding. It was perhaps caused by the mood of the day. She hoped so. Yet she had to admit that she had no idea what lay ahead of her. Somewhere up there, in those endless peaks, was Lobo.

She shook her head in anger. She had to remember to call him by his given name — Matthew. But would he remember that? It was a long time since he'd had any contact with the world of his father. Perhaps the stories she had heard were true. That he had become like an animal. Wilder than any Apache. Was she risking her life for nothing? Would he even listen to her? Would he attack her? For all she knew he might not recognise her. Elizabeth's mind whirled with confused and conflicting thoughts. Whatever the outcome, she had to try. It had been her father's dying wish that she try to do something for Matthew. Despite all the terrible news that had reached them about Matthew her father had refused to lose faith in his son. Though ill and too weak to make the attempt himself he had begged Elizabeth to make the trip on his behalf. Though he was now dead and she was on her own, Elizabeth felt obliged to honour her promise, no matter what the cost to herself.

Yet now, as she struggled along the storm-ravaged mountain slope, she felt a moment of doubt. Was she doing the right thing? Why should she succeed where the Army *and* the Apaches had failed? Would being Matthew's half-sister be enough to draw him away from his path to self-destruction?

Elizabeth felt alone and helpless, aware that perhaps she had set her hopes too high. She regretted leaving the camp, wishing she was back with Jason Brand. He was a hard and violent man, often abrupt with her. But while she had been under his protection she had felt secure. And he knew the country, could gauge the mood of the mountains. He was a man who could survive in this savage land. Yet she had turned her back on him, riding out on her own in a moment of insecurity, stranding herself in mountainous country that was both strange and alien to her.

Dragging her reluctant horse she struggled up the treacherous slope. The soft earth had turned to clinging mud that gripped her boots, pulling her back. She fell often, each time finding it harder to climb to her feet. She felt wet and cold and hungry. Leaving camp while Brand slept she had forfeited the chance of hot food and drink. She had a canteen of water and a little of the meat he had given her, but there was no chance of even stopping for that while the storm held.

Somehow she reached the top of the slope and found herself at one end of a deep valley. Her way still lay to the east. On the highest slope of the San Andres, her father had told her, was where she might find Matthew. On a flat peak that overlooked the great White Sands Desert on the far side of the mountain range. On this peak there was a high rockface. A towering cliff, and in it there was an opening that led to a hidden basin. It was a place her father had discovered himself many years ago. The only other person he had shown it to had been Matthew.

Elizabeth climbed back into the saddle and gently urged her horse across the valley floor. High overhead, near the dark peaks, she saw brilliant flashes of lightning spear into the dark sky. She felt the horse shudder, hesitate, and she was forced to hold the reins with a firm hand. Something made her look to the side. As lightning flashed again she felt sure she saw a horse and rider close by. For a moment she imagined it was Jason Brand. But that could not be. He was far below her, perhaps still trying to find her trail. So if there had been a rider — who was it?

Thunder crashed, rolling away across the valley. In its wake she thought she heard a horse snort. Elizabeth reined in, peering through the mist of rain, and sensed a dark shape looming beside her. She instinctively reached for the rifle at her knee. A large hand slid from the gloom and grasped her wrist cruelly, forcing her to bite back a pained cry.

"Easy now, sister! Ain't no sinners needing redemption just now!"

The voice was familiar. Too familiar. And when the next flash of lightning lit the area Elizabeth found herself staring into the grinning face of Preacher Jude.

His booming laugh filled her ears.

"It is providence that has brought us together, sister, and so we will stay now. You and I, and my companions, Brother Kimble and Brother Parrish."

With a burst of strength Elizabeth broke Jude's grip. She snatched up her reins and tried to turn her horse aside. Jude was too fast for her. One hand grabbed her reins. The other swept across and struck her a heavy blow on the side of her head, pitching Elizabeth from the saddle. She hit the ground hard, the breath driven from her. As she lay on the wet, muddy earth she tasted blood in her mouth.

"Learn your lesson and learn it quickly, Elizabeth Henty. Obey me or you will surely suffer."

Elizabeth heard Jude's distant voice clearly. What registered more than anything else was the use of her real name. He knew who she was, and the knowledge frightened her.

Rough hands dragged her to her feet. Jude appeared before her, his bearded face wet from the driving rain. Without a word he slapped her across the face, back and forth until her head swam and her flesh burned with pain. His blows were hard and she would have fallen if she had not been held upright.

"Ease off, Preacher," a voice called from the gloom. "Don't mark her up too much. Nights up here get colder'n a witch's tit, and this one will warm a man's blanket right well."

The voice of the man holding Elizabeth broke in. "Hell, Kimble, she'll warm more than a *blanket*."

Elizabeth's anger blotted out her pain as she struggled against the hands holding her.

"Damn you, let go! What is it you want?"

"Sister, don't play me for a fool," Jude snapped. He thrust his dripping face close to hers. "You're here looking for that half-breed brother of yours. And so am I!"

A jolt of fear went through her. She stared at Jude's angry face. His eyes burned into hers with an expression of ill disguised lust, and she was more frightened than she had ever been in her life.

"*You want to kill him!*" she said, surprised at her own calmness.

Jude smiled, relaxing a little as he straightened up. "Sister, you have seen the light."

"Why do you want him dead?"

Behind her the man gripping her arms laughed. It was an ugly, unpleasant sound.

"Tell her, Jude."

Lightning flickered above the high peaks. Wind drove fresh sheets of rain along the valley, lashing the figures grouped at the far end.

"Because, sister, he's worth 30,000 dollars to me," Jude said.

"Reward money? That's why you're here." Elizabeth's face hardened. "And you call him an *animal*."

Jude glared at her. "Do not anger me, sister. I have need of you now, but do not test my patience."

"If you think I'm going to lead you to him then you've made a big mistake, Jude." Elizabeth lifted her head and looked Jude in the eye. "I came to help him. Don't expect me to lead you to him so you can murder him."

Jude struck her without warning. This time his hand was bunched into a massive fist that caught her across the side of the face. The force of the blow drove her sideways, loosening the grip of the man holding her. Elizabeth crashed to the ground, a single cry of pain coming from her. She lay still and silent after that, fighting against the numbing pain that engulfed her face.

"Heed my words, sister," Jude yelled. "Do my bidding or face my wrath."

Strong fingers knotted in her hair, jerking her head up. Elizabeth stared into Jude's face.

"I will not be cheated out of my reward," he snarled. His features were dark with emotion. "Sister, you will take me to where this Lobo hides himself, or I will surely destroy you!"

8

THE storm ran its course, discharged its raw fury, and ended. By the middle of the morning it was as if there had never been a storm. The dark clouds rolled away and the sun burst forth, flooding the land with heat. The thirsty land sucked in the moisture and for a time the barren landscape was alive with greenery. The cycle was continuous, being repeated at intervals, going through the age-old patterns with total disregard for the machinations of man . . .

Above the valley where Elizabeth Henty had run into Preacher Jude, on a narrow ledge that ran the length of the valley's rim, squatted a motionless figure.

He wore faded buckskins that clung to his muscled, powerful legs, knee-high *n'deh b'keh*, the traditional Apache moccasin boots, and a tight dark blue shirt stolen from the body of a soldier. Dark hair hung to his strong shoulders, held back from his face by a plain red headband. The face itself was burned dark by the sun. It was hard-featured, impassive, only the eyes moving as they scanned the terrain spread before him. They searched constantly for movement, any hint that there might be others on the mountain slopes. Around his lean waist was a gunbelt and holster. A Colt revolver lay in the holster. The gunbelt's loops were filled with .44-40 cartridges, the brass shellcases glinting in the sunlight. The bullets fitted both the Colt and the Winchester held in the watcher's hands. There was also a bandolier of extra ammunition looped across his chest. More .44-40 loads. Close inspection of the bullets would have shown that the lead tip of each had been deeply marked with a cross; on impact these bullets would spread and expand, causing terrible, mushrooming wounds as they drove deep into human flesh. In a sheath attached to the gunbelt was a heavy bladed knife, its blade honed to razor sharpness.

The watcher, apparently satisfied there were no other visitors, turned his attention back to the four riders. He had been following their progress for almost an hour as they moved out of the valley and up the next rise of slopes. He was aware that no one had ever reached this far into his domain before. Soon they would be within reach of his stronghold. Before that happened he would kill them — all of them — the woman too. He could do that any time he wanted. Curiosity stayed his hand for the time being. He could guess why the men had come. He knew about the rewards. The large amount of money waiting for anyone who could bring him in dead or alive. What intrigued him was the woman's presence. Why was she here? Even at his distance from them he had realised the woman was being forced to go with the men. Yet before that she *had* been travelling on the mountain. He wondered who she was. The curiosity was short-lived. In the end she would die along with the men. Though he might use her for his own pleasure first. It had been a long time since he had been with a woman — any woman. This one looked to be young and strong. There would be ample time for him to feed the urges that rose within him. And when he tired of her she could die.

Now he rose to his full height. Tall for an Apache. Six feet. And though he wore traditional garb and his skin had been burned by the sun, there was a contrast in his features that revealed differences. The eyes were blue — pale and bitter. The facial bone structure was finer, slimmer than the classical Apache formation. Here was a man born of two races who walked a solitary path, belonging to neither white or red. In his makeup was a blend of opposing cultures, differing outlooks.

To the young woman he had been watching — though he was as yet unaware of the connection — he was blood kin. A half-brother who *she* knew as Matthew. He had long since rejected any connection with his former name and identity, as he had with the Apache half of his personality. He owed no allegiance to either race. He was himself, a man alone, seeking no company, no friends. He was looked on as an outcast by white and Apache, so he took that path. He walked in no man's shadow. Took no counsel save his own, and within those boundaries he was content. His overwhelming desire was for vengeance against anyone who came within his reach. Shunned by the world because of an accident of birth, where no guilt attached to himself, he had allowed his enforced loneliness to fester into bitterness, and now he saw all men as his enemies. They were to be destroyed. Eliminated, and he would pursue that cause until the day came when *they* killed him.

He was Lobo!

The striker of terror in the hearts of men. His name turned women pale when they were told of his horrendous deeds. Errant children were cautioned to behave lest Lobo came and took them in the dead of night. He came and went at will. Burning, looting, murdering. He knew a hundred trails that were not marked on maps. He knew every place there was water. Places to hide that even the Apache could not find. He had made the land his. It protected and fed him. Gave him water and shelter. He was as one with the land. An equal, and he made it work for him.

Silently now he moved along the narrow ledge, sure footed, his eyes never once leaving the distant figures. He moved with caution, without haste. There was no need to hurry. He knew exactly how long it would take to reach the far end of the ledge. It would place him directly above the spot where the riders would eventually pass. It was the only way out of the valley, and for Lobo the ideal place for an ambush. They would be in a narrow defile. A difficult place to traverse at the best of times. Once within the confines of the narrow place they would be unable to turn back. He would be able to kill the men and take the woman captive.

He was close to the far end of the valley when he saw one of the three men break away from the group and head back down the valley. Lobo paused, watching and wondering why this one was leaving. He raised his rifle, then held back. If he fired on this one it would warn the others. He saw no point in giving them any advantage. A shot would scatter them, making his task that much harder. He lowered the rifle and watched the lone rider tracking back along the valley floor. Better to let this one go free for now. He could concern himself with this rider later. For now he would follow his original plan and deal with the main group. Kill the men and take the girl.

She might possibly be able to tell him where the lone rider had gone. In just under an hour the group would reach the defile and start to climb. Then he would have them under his gun. By that time the lone rider would be too far away to be able to help them.

Lobo squatted and rested, his keen eyes narrowed against the sun's glare as he followed the progress of the group below. His hand absently stroked the smooth, much-used barrel of the rifle. *Soon*, he thought, *it would speak again for him, as it had done so many times before*. It would carry out his need to destroy his enemies. He sat back against the rocky slope, a cold smile touching the corners of his hard mouth as he observed the three riders moving inexorably towards his waiting trap.

9

BRAND kept moving despite the fury of the unexpected storm. The downpour washed away Elizabeth's tracks, but luckily Brand knew the general direction she was going. He was spurred on by the fact that he had seen other tracks. And before the rain washed them away he realised they were trailing Elizabeth. The tracks had been made by shod horses, not the unshod ponies that the Apache preferred. And Nante had promised to take his people away from the mountains.

The only other name Brand could think of was Preacher Jude. If it was Jude he had company — the tracks had indicated three riders.

Brand drove his horse on up the wet slopes. The wind was pushing the rain hard. It slapped at his exposed face and clawed at his sodden clothes. Despite the downpour he kept moving, aware that time was important. Elizabeth had a good start on him. He angled east, knowing that this would be the direction she would take. He tried to put himself in her place, picking the kind of terrain she would take. His horse struggled and stumbled its way over rock and crumbling ridges, across slanting beds of loose talus. Overhead the sky remained dark and brooding, streaked with heavy cloud. The wind swirled down off the high peaks and lightning seared the gloom. Thunder rolled in, rumbling angrily before building to an ear-splitting crash.

More than once Brand was forced to dismount and lead his horse across some awkward stretch. The higher he got the fiercer the storm became. He was cold and wet, his body aching from fighting the pull and drag of the wind. The skin of his face was chilled and raw, his eyes stinging.

Finally though he felt a lessening in

the storm's force. The rain began to ease off and the wind dropped. The storm was blowing itself out. It was the only thing to be said in favour of these high country storms. They didn't happen very often and when they did they exhausted themselves quickly. As the storm abated Brand was able to push his horse along at a faster rate. The sun broke through the dark clouds. It was a relief. No matter how clever man figured himself to be, he was left standing around worse than useless before the might of a storm. There wasn't a damn thing he could do to halt or even slow the raw power of nature. At the end of the day man was a pretty weak species.

As the storm faded and the hard beat of the sun spread across the land, Brand searched for any sign that might tell him who had passed this way. He saw nothing. He was expecting too much, too soon. It would probably be some time before he saw any fresh tracks. He contented himself with simply pushing forward. Gaining ground. This particular stretch of the mountain was the only access to the next slope. Elizabeth would have had no choice but to have come this way.

An hour passed. Another half. Brand was high up now. Behind him the mountain fell away in a series of undulating slopes, ridged and cut in a mixture of brown and green. The clothes that had earlier been wet from the rain were now sweatsoaked.

He drew rein, took his canteen and drank. As he replaced the canteen, bending forward to hook it over the saddle horn he saw his horse's ears flicker as they picked up a disturbance close by. It's head arced to the right. Brand didn't wait to see what had unsettled it. He slipped his feet from the stirrups and rolled out of the saddle, dropping down the horse's left side. The crack of a rifle shot followed him down. He put out his left hand to break his fall, his right dragging the heavy Colt from its holster. Hitting the ground in a crouch he sprawled belly down, eyes searching for the source of the shot.

Yards away a jumble of tumbled rock offered cover for a rifleman. It was the only likely spot he could see. Even as he scanned the area he was rewarded by a sudden movement. The tip of a rifle barrel poked out between two angled stones, then the tip of a hat.

Show yourself, you son of a bitch, Brand begged.

The rifleman remained out of sight. Probably waiting for Brand to move himself.

Time dragged.

Brand's horse wandered across the empty slope.

The sun burned through Brand's shirt.

He decided he'd done enough lying around, waiting, and gathered himself for a move. Pushing up off the ground he ran for the rocks. He expected some kind of reaction from the rifleman. Nothing happened. He reached the rocks and flattened himself against the lower section, back to the sunbaked boulders. He strained to hear any sound that would tell him where the rifleman was. For a second he wondered if the man had slipped away, but dismissed the notion because he would have seen him break clear. He was about to move again when he *did* pick up a soft scrape of sound. Boot leather against rough textured stone.

The rifleman was changing position. Now he heard the ping of a rifle barrel touching stone. The man's breathing. Closer than he had imagined. A shadow detached itself from the outline of the rocks, lengthening as the man leaned forward to get a better look. The shadow broke free from the rocks as the rifleman stepped into the open. Brand caught a swift impression of hard leanness, a thin face with small bright eyes.

The rifleman's head snapped round

as *he* sensed Brand's closeness. The lean body twisted violently as the man ducked in under Brand's raised Colt. A boney shoulder slammed into Brand's chest, pushing him back a step. He saw the man swinging the rifle clublike. He turned, taking the blow across the back of his shoulders. Grunting with pain Brand lashed out with a booted foot, catching the rifleman in the groin. The man yelled in agony, stumbling awkwardly, his face white. He still tried to bring the rifle into play. Brand gave him no chance. He levelled the Colt and pulled the trigger. The rifleman spun away, driven by the force of the .45 calibre bullet. He fell over backwards, landing heavily on the ground. A harsh rattle burst from his throat, followed by a froth of blood.

Brand kicked aside the dropped rifle. He crouched beside the man and removed his holstered handgun. As he did the small eyes focussed on him.

"*Goddam*!" the man muttered. "I ain't walkin' away from this one!"

"You wrote the rules," Brand said. He had noticed the steady stream of blood pulsing from the ragged chest wound. "Jude send you?"

The man grinned, showing yellow teeth that were stained with blood. "Maybe I don't know anybody called Jude."

"Suit yourself," Brand said and stood up. "I'll find out."

The man tried to sit up. The effort was too much and he fell back, coughing harshly, "Where the hell you goin'?"

"Up there," Brand said, gesturing toward the high peaks.

"Damn it, mister, I'm dying."

Gathering his horse's reins Brand swung into the saddle. His face was bleak as he looked down at the man. "Don't let me stop you," he said and rode on.

As he topped the next rise the man's cursing stopped abruptly. Brand urged his horse on. He did not look back. A while later he reined in at the mouth of the valley that led off from the slope he had just climbed. The deep rift stretched before him, wide and silent and deserted. He spent long minutes studying the terrain before he rode in. This seemed to be the only access to the next section of the mountain. Somewhere in the valley he would find the way.

He pushed his horse faster now, giving the animal the opportunity to run after all the hard going.

Elizabeth's image filled his mind. He wondered if she was all right. Despite his original intention not to become involved he *was* concerned. He was just as worried over her safety as he was determined to get Lobo.

His mission was Lobo. Brand hadn't forgotten that. It was just that circumstances had diverted him from his main objective. It might turn out that the half-breed was now aware of the activity in the area. If he was

Lobo would stay in the background, watching and waiting until everything was in his favour. It was the way the half-breed had built his reputation. By remaining cautious. Evaluating each set of circumstances before committing himself. And then striking when least expected.

Brand's eyes were drawn to a set of tracks. He judged they were no more than a couple of hours old. They ran ahead of him along the valley floor. The line of travel told him he had been right. This was the way out of the valley. He pushed his horse on, seeking the place that would allow him to climb to the higher slopes.

The tracks told him something else. Unless he had read them wrong it seemed certain now that Elizabeth had met someone. And Brand felt even more certain that someone had been Preacher Jude.

Just what was Jude up to? What was he looking for in these mountains?

More to the point — who was he looking for?

Brand was sure it was Lobo. But for a different purpose.

The rattle of distant gunfire broke the silence. It came from ahead of Brand, higher up the valley. Among the shots was a sound Brand recognised.

The heavy boom of Jude's big Sharps.

The firing continued in fits and starts.

Brand reached the far end of the valley and saw the narrow defile that had to be the way out.

The continuing gunfire was loud now, echoing between the rocky walls of the valley. Brand dismounted, taking his rifle. He led his horse to a sheltered spot at the mouth of the defile, then slipped in himself. Edging around a tall outcropping of shattered stone he looked along the defile. It was narrow, twisted, the sides almost sheer. The floor was strewn with debris and lay in shadow except for a few odd patches of bright sunlight.

Brand moved along the defile, the Winchester cocked and ready. His eyes searched the way ahead, and he found himself wondering just what he was going to find.

10

"**D**AMN *it, preacher, I didn't count on this!*"

Jude glanced across at Kimble. He kept his own anger under control. He admitted to himself that he hadn't expected to become trapped by Lobo himself. It wasn't supposed to work that way. Jude didn't panic. They were in a tight spot right now, but that would change. He had total confidence in his own ability. He'd crawled out of worse spots than this, and he'd do it again.

Lobo had picked his place well. The narrow defile was ideal for an ambush. Once the breed had opened fire they had been forced to vacate their saddles quickly, finding what cover they could among the tumbled rocks that littered the ground. Lobo himself was high overhead, able to take his time picking his targets. One of the problems Jude and Kimble were finding was the bright sun that struck them full in the face. It made pinpointing Lobo difficult, even though he was constantly moving back and forth along the clifftop.

The half-breed had kept them pinned down for a couple of hours now. Only a stroke of luck had allowed them to reach cover before one of Lobo's initial shots had struck home. Lobo's first shot had struck Kimble's horse, burning it across the flank. Since then a steady exchange of fire had taken place, neither side hitting anything. Jude knew that Lobo was in the best position. They were safe as long as they stayed under cover. If they made a break he could pick them off easily. He had them trapped and he could keep them under his waiting gun for as long as he wanted.

Kimble was aware of the situation too. The realisation angered and frightened him. He was stuck behind a rock with no place to go. Sitting with his back to the rock wall he digested the facts. On the one hand there was Lobo, a half-breed crazy man, just waiting to blow his head off. Then there was Jude. The more he thought about it the more he was convinced Jude was just as crazy as the breed. What with all his damn bible spouting. It was Jude who had talked Kimble and Parrish into joining in this stupid hunt for Lobo. The promised one third share of the reward money seemed a long way off to Kimble now. The way things were changing he wasn't going to get much out of this deal.

Unless!

Kimble thought about the girl. She had ducked under cover the moment the shooting started. Now she was huddled in a cleft of rock. Kimble could see her, but he couldn't get to her. He glanced in her direction, eyeing her boldly, and deciding that his first appraisal of her had been right. She *was* a good looking female. She would be worth taking. Kimble realised she would put up a hell of a fight — but that was all part of the game. The hell with a passive woman who didn't resist. Kimble liked his ladies to have spirit. He began to feel uncomfortable, aware that it was his desire for her that was doing it. There she was. So close — and unattainable. He silently cursed the man called Lobo. His anger gathered suddenly and he raised his rifle, emptying it at the clifftop, blinking his eyes against the dazzling sunlight.

"*Save your ammunition!*" Jude yelled across the gap that separated them. "He wants us to panic. Hold back your anger lest it makes a fool of you!"

"Jude, shut your goddam mouth!" Kimble raged. "I am mighty sick of listening to that horseshit you keep peddling. You're no more a damn preacher than my horse's ass!"

"Brother Kimble, I will overlook your words," Jude droned tonelessly. "In your desperation you are not responsible for your words."

"Shit, you goddam fake!" Kimble

113

screamed. He jabbed a finger in Jude's direction. "Damned if I can figure why I let myself get talked into comin' up here. Christ, I could be back in Gallego, sharing that Mex woman's bed, and having a hell of a time. What the hell am I doing stuck halfway up a mountain being shot at by a loco half-breed? Jude, you must be crazy if you think we're goin' to collect that reward. Ain't nobody ever going to stop that breed."

"*No!*" Jude thundered. His control was slipping now, anger forcing its way to the surface. "You are weak, Kimble. Undeserving of my generosity. I promised you a share of the reward. I picked you and Parrish off the streets of Gallego when you had nothing!"

"Well ain't that the horse's ass! Jude, you pissant, it don't make no difference how big that reward is if we're all dead."

Jude's face darkened. Almost without conscious thought he swung the big Sharps in Kimble's direction, his finger easing back against the trigger. Kimble held his stare, sensing Jude's wild state, well aware that he was close to death. He gripped his own rifle, bringing it to bear on Jude. He wasn't about to let Jude get away with such a move . . .

And then Jude turned the rifle's muzzle away from Kimble, directing it at a point behind the man. A second later the heavy crash of the Sharps filled the defile, the noise thunderous in the close area.

Kimble twisted about, his eyes seeking Jude's target. He picked up a moving figure. A tall man, dark haired and clad in dusty trail clothes. He was strongly built, his brown face strong boned and determined. As Kimble focussed on him he saw the man throw himself to one side as the .50 calibre bullet exploded savagely against hard rock, filling the air with stone chips.

"*Brand*!" Jude yelled. "It's Brand!"

So this was Jason Brand! A thought occurred to Kimble — if Brand was here he must have got by Parrish. And the only way he would have done that would have been by killing him. A seething rage boiled up in Kimble. He had partnered Parrish for a long time. Now this man had most likely killed him.

Kimble forgot the danger that lurked overhead. It slipped from his mind as he shoved to his feet, lifting his rifle to line it up on the distant figure of Jason Brand.

Kimble didn't hear the bullet that killed him. His finger was already pulling back on the trigger when something struck him a terrific blow at the back of his skull. As the initial impact was still registering, the bullet that caused it — driving down from the clifftop — tore its way through flesh and bone and into Kimble's brain. The expanding chunk of lead caused terrible and terminal damage. Kimble experienced a moment of white hot pain before darkness swallowed him. He was dead before his body struck the ground.

Even while Kimble was falling Jude, his Sharps reloaded, forced himself to remain calm. He turned by reflex, swinging up the heavy gun. For once Lobo had exposed himself more than usual, and his own bulk partially blocked out the bright glare of the sun. Jude located his target, held the figure for a fraction, then touched the trigger. The big Sharps kicked back, the muzzle blasting flame and smoke, spitting a massive .50 calibre bullet out at tremendous speed.

Overhead the dark shape jerked sideways, stumbled for a moment, then straightened up and vanished from sight.

Jude felt a surge of excitement. He didn't know how badly — but he knew he'd hit Lobo. He had done what no other man had ever done. He had put a bullet in the half-breed. He smiled to himself. The reward suddenly wasn't so far out of reach after all!

11

CONFUSION reigned.

Brand used it to his advantage. Seeing Kimble go down, his skull blown apart by one of Lobo's bullets, and Jude's swift reaction, he saw his own — fleeting — opportunity.

While Jude was attempting to reload Brand ran along the defile. He had already spotted Elizabeth, and she had seen him. Before he could warn her to stay put she came out from cover and moved to meet him. Her action placed her between Brand and Jude, blocking Brand's clear shot at the man.

Jude became aware of Brand's closeness. He made a strangled sound deep in his throat, turning to face the advancing lawman. Abandoning his attempt to reload his rifle Jude gripped the Sharps by the barrel, lunging forward.

Brand, unable to use the Winchester

because of Elizabeth, closed in fast. He shouldered Elizabeth aside roughly, ducking under the swinging Sharps and slamming bodily into Jude. Jude staggered aside, stumbling to his knees. Following through Brand swept the butt of the Winchester round, clouting Jude across the side of the face. The hard wood struck with a sickening thud, driving Jude to the ground. Jude hit on his face and lay still, blood staining his thick beard.

Brand turned back to Elizabeth. He caught hold of her arm and yanked her upright, pushing her along the defile. As he did a shot rang out from the clifftop. Lobo was still around, and able to fight back, despite being hit. The bullet slammed into the ground inches behind Brand. Ignoring Elizabeth's protests he kept her moving. He wanted to get them into some kind of cover. Away from Lobo's rifle. A stream of bullets followed them, chipping rock and hissing through the air close by. None of them found their intended

119

target save one that scored a bloody gash across the top of Elizabeth's left shoulder. She gave a gasp, stumbling. Brand gripped her arm and pulled her upright, practically dragging her along,

Then they were in a kind of tunnel, formed by the coming together of the opposing walls of the defile. The inward curve of the rock formed a natural roof. It closed them off from the cliffs overhead. For the moment they were safe, but Brand didn't expect it to last.

He pushed Elizabeth against the side wall. Propped himself beside her. They dragged air into their lungs. Sweat trickled down their faces, stinging eyes and tasting salty on their lips. After a few moments Elizabeth allowed herself to slide to the ground. She stared up at Brand, not speaking, and for the first time he was able to see her face clearly. Someone had given her a hard time. One side of her face was badly bruised. She had a gash over one eye.

"Jude?" he asked.

Her hand automatically reached up to cover the bruising. "I had to tell him," she said vaguely; she wasn't speaking to Brand — for a moment her mind was wandering. "He would have killed me."

Brand took her arm again and pulled her to her feet. "It might still happen," he growled. Still half-dragging her he moved on along the tunnel. It began to curve away to the left. Brand held the rifle ready in case Lobo showed himself. The half-breed could still be around. There was no way of telling how badly he had been hit by Jude's bullet. It hadn't stopped him, and as long as he was able to handle a gun Lobo would be a threat.

Thinking about threats Brand realised he had made a mistake leaving Jude alive. He should have killed the man there and then. But he had been determined to get Elizabeth out of harm's way. A mistake, allowing sentiment to get in the way of practicality. Once Jude recovered from

Brand's blow he would be on their tail again.

The tunnel roof opened up. Bright shafts of sunlight speared down into the defile. Brand held back, searching the way ahead. Another ten yards and the defile came to a dead end. He saw a place where the sheer wall of the defile gave way to a steep, but passable slope. It would allow them to reach the clifftop where Lobo had fired down on them.

"Can you climb?" he asked Elizabeth.

She stared at him. Her eyes were still dull. "Climb!" she echoed.

Brand turned her towards the slope. The way was rough and hard. Brand had to push Elizabeth ahead of him, while keeping his eyes open for any sign of movement.

They climbed slowly, Elizabeth still awkward in her movements. Dazed. She had obviously been badly shaken by the incident in the defile, and the shock of the bullet graze had left its mark.

It was the longest climb Brand had ever made. If Lobo was still around and decided to start shooting, he would have two easy targets. In the event the renegade didn't show. Nor did Jude.

Finally, gasping for every breath, bodies aching and bruised, and sodden with sweat Brand and Elizabeth reached the top. They struggled over the final few feet and found they were at the top of the cliff. The defile lay far below them. Brand could see the sprawled figure of Kimble. There was no sign of Jude. To the right and in the distance he could see the broad sweep of the valley.

Elizabeth had slumped to the ground. She rolled face down, her body heaving with exertion. Brand could see the tear in her blouse where the bullet had caught her. Fresh blood overlaid the original dark stain.

Brand hefted the Winchester, turned and studied the mass of rock that rose behind them. This was the highest point in this section of the San

Andres. There were higher peaks, though they lay miles to the north. Here, on this level plateau they only had this jutting peak rising some two-hundred feet above them. He studied it closely. It spread for maybe a mile or so across the plateau, running more or less from north to south. From this position there was no telling how deep it actually was. The first fifty feet was a sheer face of rock, the surface split and weathered.

He helped Elizabeth to her feet and she followed him without protest. Brand stood at the rockface. The final approach was across a long slope layered with loose shale and dotted with hefty chunks of weathered rock. When they reached the rockface Elizabeth put her back to it and slid to the ground.

"I don't care what you say, Brand, I can't go any further."

"Maybe we won't have to," he said.

She raised her head, pushing tangled

hair away from her face. "What are you talking about?"

Brand crouched in front of her. "You know damn well what I'm talking about," he said sharply. "The reason we're all here. You, me, and Jude. Your half brother. Lobo."

The dullness faded from Elizabeth's eyes, replaced by anger. "How did you know?"

"I've known all the time," he told her. "It's my job to know."

"You tricked me!" she said bitterly. "Damn you, Jason Brand, you tricked me!"

"I did what I had to," he said. "No more than you with your phoney name and husband."

"My reasons were my own," she said lamely. Then bitingly she snapped: "And what are you? Another damned bounty hunter like Jude?"

Brand shook his head. "I'm not after any reward."

"Then what?" Awareness came to her even as she spoke. "The law!

125

You're the law. You want to take him back and hang him!"

"Something has to be done to stop him."

"But why must . . . " Her voice trailed away. She was empty of words.

"Elizabeth, I understand your need to try and help him. But I think he's beyond that now. He won't quit. He can't. It's gone too far."

"All I wanted was to talk with him. To get him to leave this place. I stood it as long as I could. Knowing who he was. Hearing all the talk about the things he's supposed to have done."

"It couldn't have been easy."

"It wasn't that so much. It was knowing I might be able to stop it. But I was too much of a coward to face the fact."

Brand reached out to touch her face. "Nobody could call you that. Not after what you've just been through."

"Have I done any good? Now I'm this close I don't believe I can do anything. From what I can see all those things I heard seem to be true."

"I wish I could tell you they weren't."

Elizabeth climbed to her feet. "No more games, Brand. We might not be in this mess if I'd been honest from the start. I'm sorry I ran out on you. But . . . I just got scared. I wanted to do it on my own. Instead I walked right into Jude's hands. And you had to pull me out of trouble again — just like you did back in Gallego. I have to thank you again."

"I was bound to meet up with Jude again sooner or later."

"If we do find Lobo — I mean Matthew — will you at least give me the chance to talk with him?"

Brand had to accept Elizabeth's courage. Despite everything that had happened she wasn't giving up. And he had to admit she had earned the right to at least give her way a try.

"All right. But only on my say so. If he won't talk and comes out shooting, you stay back if I tell you. Maybe I don't have your faith in human nature. I don't take anyone on trust. My job is to deal with the situation whichever way it goes. I'll take Lobo alive if I can. But I'm not risking my life — or yours — just for a whim. One wrong move and I'll kill him."

Elizabeth nodded. "Hard as it is to accept, I agree, Mr Brand."

"It's Jason."

Her eyes smiled for a brief moment. "My friends call me Liz."

Brand studied the sky. "Going to be dark soon. We need somewhere to rest up. This is no place to be wandering round at night. And it gets damn cold too."

He passed her the rifle, slipping the Colt into his hand.

"Stay here. Keep your eyes open. You see anything move, you shoot. Don't play games. You lose it up here you lose it for good."

"I'll be fine," she said, handling the rifle with the ease of someone who knew how to use it.

Brand moved along the rockface. There was something about it that had caught his interest. He wasn't certain what it was at first, and as he checked out the rock he began to wonder if he had been mistaken. It looked like a hundred other rockfaces, eroded by thousands of years of harsh weather. And then he saw it. A narrow slit in the rock. At first glance it looked like any of the other splits in the face. When he looked closer he saw that this one cut deeper into the rock. The line of the split was at such an acute angle that it could easily be missed. Standing to the side he saw that the crack angled far into the rockface. A jolt of excitement coursed through him. Brand crouched and inspected the ground at the base of the split. There were faint scuff marks in the rock under the dust. Brushing away the dirt he saw that the rock had been worn smooth. Someone was using the place regularly. *Lobo*? Was this the entrance to the renegade's hideout? The hidden refuge that had remained undiscovered for so long? Brand straightened up and eased into the opening. It was wide enough to allow a horse through. He walked in a few yards and saw the passage opened up. Ahead it curved off to the right. Brand returned to the entrance and stepped out.

Elizabeth was a few yards away, searching for him with frightened eyes. She gasped when he suddenly reappeared.

"Where did you go?"

Brand showed her the opening.

"It's just how my father described it," she admitted, explaining what her father had told her, "Are we going in?"

"At least we'll have shelter."

"Matthew may be in there."

"I thought about that too."

They moved into the passage, Brand in the lead. The rock walls reared up on either side, towering high over their heads. The faces were smooth and unbroken. The passage ran on in a series of right and left bends, but always pushing deeper into the bulk of the rock. It cut its way for a quarter of a mile, then suddenly opened out in a wide, oval basin. It was surrounded on all sides by the sheer walls of the mountain. At its widest point it was easily a couple of miles across. Water glinted in the sunlight. It came from a fissure high in one wall, spilling into a deep, wide pool. Small streams meandered across the basin, spidering out from the pool. Because of the water the basin floor was a patchwork of greenery. Stands of pine rose in the shadow of the rock walls and grass carpeted large areas of the basin floor.

"It is exactly how father described it," Elizabeth said again. "Even the waterfall and the pool. It has to be Matthew's place."

"Ideal for what he needs. Well hidden. Little chance of visitors. Water. Grass. Timber. Probably game too. And an easy place to defend."

They crossed the basin. The silence was almost soothing. The place caught the warmth of the setting sun.

Brand noticed tracks now. Hoofprints. Here and there the outline of soft-soled moccasins.

This had to be Lobo's hideout. The sanctuary of the half-breed. The wolf's lair.

They followed the tracks across the basin, nearing the pool. And found Lobo's cave.

The entrance was the height of a man. Close by was a small lean-to and a split-pole corral. Two sturdy ponies moved restlessly around the fenced area. Just in front of the cave entrance was a shallow firepit; Brand felt the black ashes and found they were cold.

"If he's back he isn't eating," he observed dryly.

Elizabeth was staring around her, anxiety showing clearly on her face.

"No telling how badly Jude hurt him. Could be he's still out there somewhere. Maybe too weak to make it back until he's rested. If he is alive he'll show up eventually. And if he does he'll know we're here."

He went into the cave to look around. It was roomy inside. Against one wall were blankets. Close by was a pile of clothing. At the rear of the cave he found a food store. There were stacked tins of food. Bottles of liquor. Hanging from poles were sacks of beans, flour, strips of dried meat. He found coffee beans too. There were weapons as well on a rawhide-bound rack. Brand counted more than a dozen rifles. As many handguns. There were leather bandoliers with filled loops. Boxes of ammunition stolen from the Army. Kegs of powder and strips of lead; there were bullet moulds and even a set of brass scales for measuring out the powder.

Apart from cooking and eating utensils there was nothing else. Nothing that suggested personal belongings, or that offered any kind of comfort against the crude surroundings. The cave was nothing more than a shelter. A place to eat and sleep and replenish supplies. A place to store the instruments of violence that ruled the life of the man called Lobo.

Elizabeth took a look inside, coming out quickly, her face pale.

"It's a terrible place, Jason. It doesn't even look as if a human lives in it. It's just like an animal's den." She turned to Brand, her eyes bleak. "There isn't even a picture. Or a book. My God, Jason, what has he become?"

Brand didn't answer. There wasn't much he could say. Elizabeth had answered her own question. There was no point hurting her by saying it to her face. The brother she had known as Matthew Henty was no more. The renegade Lobo had taken his place. Driven by hate, with a desire to maim and to kill. With the basic instinct of some primaeval beast Lobo needed to destroy. He only lived to bring death to any human who crossed his path.

The years of injustice and prejudice had pushed him beyond the limits — too far for any kind of return to normality.

Elizabeth's desire to help her brother seemed more of a lost cause now. Brand wished he could ease her out of the hurt that was bound to come. But she was committed, and hurt or no, she *would* try to get through to Matthew Henty.

Brand had never felt more helpless. He could see the hurt coming. Could imagine what it would do to her. And he couldn't do a damn thing to stop it.

12

THE fire Brand had made cast warm splashes of orange light into the cave entrance. He had food and coffee hung over the flames. Beyond the cave entrance the basin lay in deep shadow. Overhead the velvet sweep of the night sky was studded with stars. There was only a pale moon. With the darkness had come a swift mountain chill, and Brand had been surprised when Elizabeth had taken a blanket, saying she was going to the pool to bathe. And she had. He could hear her splashing in the water, thinking that only a woman would do such a thing, chancing a dip in ice cold water. The diversion would probably help her to temporarily forget her problems.

Lifting the coffee pot off the flames Brand poured himself a mug full. He wondered if Lobo was out in the darkness somewhere. Maybe watching and waiting. He might still be out on one of the cold mountain slopes, hurt and sick. Or dead. Somehow the final option didn't ring true. Brand figured he wasn't about to get so lucky. He thought about Jude, too. Where was the man?

He pushed the thoughts to the back of his mind. He would know soon enough when something happened. There was no point in him sitting and worrying over the pair all night. He was too hungry and tired. Not that he didn't need to stay alert. That was something he did without conscious thought. It was bred into him — a natural phenomenon akin to breathing. He would remain concerned over Lobo and Jude, but it wouldn't prevent him from getting the food and rest he needed.

He heard Elizabeth coming back to the cave. It was, he realised the sound of her bare feet he had picked up, and not the noise of her boots. She approached the fire. She carried her clothes in a bundle and had the blanket wrapped around her. Dropping the bundle she sat down by the fire. Brand poured her a mug of coffee and she took it gratefully,

"Was that water cold!" she exclaimed. Her eyes were enormous in the dancing firelight and Brand could see water droplets in her dark hair. She lowered the mug. "I feel better though."

"How's the shoulder?"

She twisted her upper body round, allowing the blanket to slip from her shoulders. Brand leaned forward to inspect the wound. It was slight. No more than a thin gouge, and it had already sealed itself off. "Stings a little is all," she said. When she turned back to the fire Brand couldn't fail to glimpse the upper curves of her smooth white breasts before she pulled the blanket close again. She caught his eye and held it, her cheeks colouring gently before she looked away with a quick:

"Jason. I'm hungry. Can we eat?"

He spooned out hot beans. He had found dried peppers among Lobo's food store. Adding them to the beans, along with some flour, he had seasoned and thickened the mixture. He watched her eat.

"I never knew beans could taste so good," she said.

"Hell, you *must* be hungry then. You want some more?"

"Well, maybe not that good," she admitted, her tone gently teasing.

Brand smiled and Elizabeth laughed softly. Even so they emptied the pot of beans and drank all the coffee between them.

More than once Brand found himself watching her. Observing her movements. He was held by her captivating beauty, and felt the demanding urge he had experienced before. Only this time it was stronger. When she moved the firelight rippled in her dark hair and stroked the smooth flesh of her face, the curve of a bare shoulder where the blanket had slipped. She would return his gaze, and when their eyes met she stared at him with an uncompromising boldness that only increased his desire for her.

A little later he walked to the pool and stripped off his shirt. He removed the bandage she had bound around his body after the gunfight in Gallego and washed the wound. It had closed nicely, though it was still tender around the edges. Washing the dust from his face and body he allowed the chill water to ease the bruises and grazes he had picked up. When he returned to the fire Elizabeth had gone. He laid down the rifle he'd taken with him and sat staring into the flames.

He heard a soft sound coming from the cave entrance, and when he turned he could see her. He retrieved the rifle and went to the entrance, following her inside. She was a pale shadow, but he sensed her closeness and could feel her warmth.

"Here," she called out of the shadows;

her tone was soft, but he sensed the urgency in her voice.

Propping the rifle against the cave wall he turned to where she stood. As he reached her she moved and a shaft of moonlight caught the pale nakedness of her smooth body. In the moment before she pressed herself to him, he caught a glimpse of softly rounded breasts and the curve of hips and long, firm thighs. Her mouth touched his, warm and soft, demanding. He held her against him, aware of his growing need for her. His strong hands moved restlessly over her supple form, touching, caressing, and Elizabeth sighed gently as she responded. She slid her hands down his body to tug at the buckle of his heavy gunbelt.

"Damn thing!" he heard her murmur before it slipped free and they eased down onto the blankets she had spread across the cave floor.

After that there was little time for talk. They were both caught up in the frantic heat of the moment, each searching for their individual need. The all too brief moment that would allow them to forget the thoughts and fears haunting them . . .

* * *

It was Elizabeth who returned them to reality some time later, lying against him under the warming blankets.

"Jason, will he come back?"

"He'll come."

The lovely body trembled against his. "I'm getting scared now," she admitted.

Brand drew her closer. Her flesh was silken and warm. He turned her face to his and kissed her. She held him, gripping him tightly, pushing herself hard against him.

"It never lasts does it?" she said.

He realised she was voicing his own thoughts. In his life he found little room for permanent relationships. His existence made life an uncertain thing, something that could end swiftly. He lived in a world of casual violence, snatching his comfort and pleasure wherever and whenever he could — just as he was doing now — and somehow Elizabeth had become aware of that state of mind.

"Just *who* do you work for, Jason?" she asked.

He couldn't help smiling, even though she couldn't see.

"People," he said, thinking of McCord and Whitehead and Kito. And all the others at the ranch outside Washington. It was the first time he had thought about them since he had talked with Alex Mundy back in Rawdon. He tried to imagine what they were doing right now. He was not aware of the events that were taking place that would eventually plunge him into his next assignment shortly after his return to Washington.

Beside him Elizabeth drifted into sleep. Brand lay for a time, listening to the night sounds. A wind had risen, pushing in from the north. It sighed through the trees growing in the basin. Whispered its way through the grass. A gust buffeted the rockface above the cave entrance, causing the fire to flare briefly. A half-burned stick toppled, sending bright sparks leaping skywards. They were caught by the wind and whipped away into the darkness. They shone for a few seconds then swiftly died and vanished.

Brand reached out and drew his Colt revolver close. He lay back, feeling Elizabeth stir in her sleep as he settled against her.

13

BRAND woke as always. Quietly, his senses quickly adjusting to his surroundings. He lay for a moment, realising he was alone under the blankets. Then he smelled coffee. Sitting upright his right hand automatically closed over the butt of the Colt, lifting it. Pale light flooded the cave and beyond the entrance he could see the dawn sky.

Now he could see Elizabeth, kneeling by the fire. The Winchester was propped against a rock close by her hand.

He rolled out of the blankets, reaching for his clothing. He dressed quickly, strapping on his gunbelt as he went outside, stamping his feet down into his boots.

Elizabeth glanced round, dark hair sliding away from her face as she looked up at him. "Coffee's almost ready."

He nodded, stepping by her, his eyes searching the spread of the basin. Nothing seemed out of place. He checked the corral. The pair of ponies looked at ease. They moved leisurely around the enclosure; if anything unusual was brewing the ponies would sense it first; they were highly-strung, sensitive creatures and were easily upset. Satisfied for the moment Brand returned to the fire where Elizabeth handed him a mug of coffee.

"I didn't want to disturb you," she said. "You were sleeping so well."

Brand might have told her why he had slept well, but he sensed she already knew seeing the way her cheeks flushed. She averted her gaze.

"It's so beautiful here," she said, almost sadly. "I almost wish Matthew wouldn't come. If he does it will all end in violence."

She looked over at him, seeing him in a different light now. Even seated, drinking coffee, his entire being was taut, prepared for any trouble that might come his way. She noted the way the holstered Colt lay against his thigh, as much a part of him as a hand or an eye. A faint shiver ran through her. He *was* different this morning. His mouth set in a hard line, his eyes holding a distant, almost hostile expression that frightened her.

"How long will you wait for him?" she asked.

He stared at her as if the question was foolish. When he spoke it was with the tone of a teacher instructing a child in the most basic of solutions to a problem.

"Until he comes," he said tonelessly.

Neither of them wanted food. Brand finished his coffee, then crossed to the corral. He stepped inside and spent some time with the ponies. Elizabeth longed to go to him, but she knew he was not in the mood for company. She wandered into the cave. The blankets they had shared lay crumpled and twisted on the ground, and she recalled the moment he had come to her in the darkness. In a rush she remembered the desire she had experienced. The longfelt need, and the almost desperate way they had satisfied those longings. Unsettled by the images in her mind Elizabeth turned and hurried out of the cave. As she stepped outside she felt the heat of the rising sun strike her.

"Stay where you are!"

Brand's voice reached her with near physical force. Sharp and commanding. He was only yards from her, the Winchester in his hands. He was looking out across the basin. Elizabeth followed his gaze and a shock ran through her. Two figures were approaching, heading in the direction of the cave, one behind the other.

The leading figure was Preacher Jude. Barely recognizable. His clothing was ripped and filthy. Dark dried blood streaked the bruised, lacerated flesh of his face. The left side resembled a hunk of raw meat. Even a part of his beard had been ripped away. Yet even now his eyes stared out from his ravaged face, the fanatical gleam undiminished.

Behind Jude, a rifle trained on his captive's spine, was Lobo.

He walked lightly, despite the wound in his left leg; Jude's shot had torn a deep gash in his upper thigh. Though the bullet hadn't lodged Lobo had lost a lot of blood before managing to hide himself away and tend the wound.

Watching the pair Brand said: "Stand back, Liz, and for God's sake don't do anything stupid."

She threw him an angry glance. "You promised I could talk to him."

"You will. If he has a mind to listen. I need to know that first."

Lobo halted some yards off. He studied the scene before him, anger rising as he realised the man and girl had stayed the night in his cave, probably using his food. He recalled the effort it had taken bringing in all the supplies, and his rage grew, though nothing showed in his eyes or on his stone face.

The prolonged silence proved too much for Jude. He was in pain from the struggle with Lobo when the half-breed had come on him in the darkness. Lobo's single-minded ferocity had overcome even Jude's brute strength. During the short confrontation Jude had been driven back over a rocky ledge. The fall had been bone-jarring, leaving Jude smashed and bleeding. Lobo had no trouble forcing the bounty hunter towards his hideout. Jude had lost much of his will to fight and Lobo's endless questions about the girl and the man — plainly Brand — had been easier to answer than to lie about. Jude was already bitter over the fact that he was the captive of the very man he had come hunting himself. His discomfort was increased when they finally arrived at Lobo's hideout to find Brand and the girl already there.

"The Lord has seen fit to curse me!" Jude said, breaking the silence. "I am surrounded by mine enemies!"

Lobo eased up close and slammed the butt of his rifle into Jude's side. Ribs cracked under the impact and Jude clasped his arms round his body, hunching over, moaning softly. Lobo jammed the rifle's muzzle against the side of his head.

"*No! Wait!*"

Elizabeth's cry burst from her lips as she ran forward.

"Listen to me, Matthew! Please don't kill him!"

Lobo's head came up and he stared at Elizabeth for a long moment. "Why are you using that name? Who are you, woman?"

Elizabeth continued to approach him.

Before Brand could react Lobo snapped the rifle to his shoulder, the muzzle levelling on Elizabeth. Brand swore to himself. His first mistake had been not to shoot Lobo the minute he had set eyes on him. Dead the renegade couldn't have hurt anyone. Now his rifle was trained on Elizabeth. There was no way Brand could get off a clear shot that would guarantee her safety.

Damn her! Why hadn't she waited? Why couldn't she have given him the time he needed? He could have taken his shot. Not that it mattered now. The damage was done.

"I asked you a question, woman. Who are you?" Lobo's voice crackled through the silence.

"I'm Elizabeth Henty. Your sister. My mother was different, but we shared our father. Daniel Henty."

Lobo gave a mirthless smile. "Sister? You are a half-sister as I am a half-breed. That is all we have in common."

"No, Matthew! We have much more. There is a bloodtie between us that words cannot change."

"*Bloodtie!*" Lobo spat into the dust. "Do you think I am a fool. Your blood is pure. I have the blood of two races in me. Apache and white. Neither accepts me, and I curse them both!"

"Listen to me, Matthew. I came

to talk. Our father is dead. Before he passed away he begged me to help you."

"Help? What help can you offer, little half-sister? I want for nothing. Everything I need is here. Food. Water. Shelter."

"My help is of a different kind. Matthew, I want you to come away from here. Give up this life. It's all just a waste."

"Ah! So you want me to surrender. To give myself up so the Army can hang me. Was it the Army who sent you?"

Elizabeth shook her head angrily. She was close to tears. "No! I came by myself. You have to believe me."

"Then who are the whites with you?" Lobo demanded, anger filling his loud voice. "If you came alone where did these two come from?"

"The law sent me," Brand said. "My job is to take you in. Any way I can. Alive or dead. The girl knew nothing about me until I told her."

Lobo smiled a predator's smile. He studied Brand for a time. "You killed the one who backtracked?"

Brand nodded. "Jude and his partners found out who the girl was. They figured she'd lead them to you so they could haul your corpse in for a 30,000 dollar bounty."

The smile faded. A shadow darkened Lobo's face. "Now I am taken notice of," he said. "But only because I can bring them money."

"Then give yourself up, Matthew," Elizabeth begged. "While you go on the way you are others will come after you. More men like Jude."

"And men like him?" Lobo said, staring at Brand.

"He's here only because of his duty. He doesn't do it for the money. He's protecting the innocent."

"Innocent?" Lobo echoed. "Of course! The good. The decent. Words with no meaning. When I tried to live in their towns it was the *good* people who despised me most of all. The men who called me a dirty breed and spat in my face. But they forgot their words when they visited the brothels and paid money to bed the half-breed whores. Are these your innocents? And their women were worse. They shrank from me in the streets with hate in their eyes. To them I was evil. They hid their children from me and told their daughters never to go near me or I would ravish them in the dirt. I had done nothing to any of them. My only crime was to be born. To live in a shadow world of hate and distrust. You ask me to give myself up to these people. I would sooner cut my own throat."

"Maybe you could have tried harder," Brand said.

"Why should I have to try harder than others? I wanted only the same chances. I did not ask for more. But I was denied even the most simple things."

"So now you figure to kill us all and have it for yourself!"

"I have chosen my path," Lobo said. He lashed out with his rifle, brutally slamming the barrel against the side of Jude's head. "As this one chose the path he walks, so have I taken my own way."

The half-breed's words and the tone of his voice told Brand all he needed to know. There was no mistaking Lobo's intentions. He would kill them all — Elizabeth included. Sister or no — Lobo would kill her without a moment's thought.

It left Brand no choice. He had to make his move there and then, because once Lobo began his deadly work there would be no chance.

He moved even as the thought crossed his mind, throwing himself forward and down, the Winchester's muzzle angling up to track Lobo's already moving form. The rifle settled on Lobo and Brand eased back on the trigger.

In the instant Brand fired Preacher Jude, reacting to Lobo's savage blow, threw himself at the half-breed, knocking him off balance. The pair tumbled to the ground in a tangle of limbs, Jude on top.

The Winchester's bullet passed harmlessly over the prone bodies.

"Liz, get the hell away from here!" Brand yelled as he pushed to his feet. He saw her turn to look in his direction, her face pale, terror-stricken. *"Go! Damn you, get out of here!"*

He ran on by her, sensing her turn away. His target was still Lobo. He heard a strangled yell from Jude, and a moment later there was the muffled boom of a handgun. Jude's bulk lifted from Lobo, twisting over as he rolled away from the renegade. There was a large, gory hole over his heart, blood pumping from it fiercely. As Jude's dead form hit the ground the front of his shirt still smouldered from the muzzle flash of the pointblank shot.

Brand triggered the Winchester when he saw that Lobo was holding a revolver as well as his own rifle.

The .44-40 bullet ripped a gout of bloody flesh from Lobo's side. The half-breed fell, rolled and came up on one knee. Brand fired again and saw this shot kick up dirt inches away from the renegade. Then the half-breed's hand swept round, the revolver glinting in the instant before it fired. Brand saw the muzzleflash, but didn't hear the shot because the bullet caught him a glancing blow across the side of the head. It was a stunning blow. It spun him round. He felt his senses leave him. He was falling before he realised. Unable to prevent it happening he gasped at the impact. The Winchester spilled from his hands. He fought against the darkness that was threatening to engulf him. Warm blood was spilling down across his face. He tasted the saltiness on his lips. His strength seemed to be draining away. Brand tried to get up, managing to wedge one arm under him. He blinked his eyes, trying to clear them. In the distance, sounding as if it was coming to him along a deep tunnel, he heard a scream. It was a high, shrill, terrified sound, and instinctively he thought of Elizabeth. He rubbed his hand over his eyes. Now he could see a little better. He scanned the area. Moved by the corral. He located the cave entrance. And saw Elizabeth. The half-breed was almost on her. Brand clawed for his Colt, pulling it free. He dogged back the hammer with a great effort. Somehow he lurched to his feet. He took two steps then went down again. That was when he heard the second scream. The utter horror of it tore him apart. He lay helpless, cursing the weakness that held him to the ground. Coming again from a far distance he picked up a sound like the pounding of hooves. He heard shouting. Gunshots. He fought to climb upright again. His mind was full of jumbled, disconnected thoughts. On his feet, lurching drunkenly, he felt a burning pain spearing into his skull. He stared around, through tear filled eyes. *Where was that damned breed*? A horse squealed. Brand swung round towards the corral. Lobo was astride one of the ponies. The corral was open and the renegade was urging his pony through the gap. Brand brought the Colt up in a clumsy arc, triggering too soon, and saw his bullet rip splinters of pale wood from one of the corner posts. He staggered in the direction of the corral. He reached the gap just as Lobo burst free. Dust billowed up from under the pony's hooves. Brand made an attempt to block its passing. His free hand caught hold of Lobo's leg, digging his fingers into the buckskin pants. He felt Lobo begin to slip from the pony's back. Lobo yelled in wild anger. Brand sensed, rather than saw, the half-breed's rifle lashing down. It struck him across the skull, pain exploding brutally. Lobo struck again. Brand fell back, letting go of Lobo's leg. The half-breed kicked out, his foot clouting Brand full in the face. He crashed heavily to the ground. This time when he tried to get up the

160

pain in his head swelled to white-hot agony and he slipped back. Far off he thought he heard someone shout. More shots — then nothing. The pain went away and the world became a silent place filled with blinding light. The light began to fade, turning to grey, then to utter blackness. This time he didn't even try to fight it. The effort was beyond him. He lay back and drifted . . .

14

AWARENESS was a long time coming. Brand was not waking from a natural sleep. His injured body had shut down, demanding to be given time to at least begin to heal itself, and there was a reluctance to remove itself from the protection of the recovery process. As he did come out of the soothing darkness and into the physical world, Brand's first response was to groan against the bands of ragged pain gripping his pounding skull. The pulsing beat had an obscene strength. Each fresh wave caused him to break out in a cold sweat of agony. He wondered if his skull was fractured. He felt nauseous, and he also felt angry at his own apparent weakness.

When he finally opened his eyes a too-bright light blinded him. He closed his eyes again, glad to be back in the darkness. He lay still, though he was restless and wanted to be on his feet. There were things to be done. Questions to be asked. He wanted to know where Elizabeth was and if she was unharmed. Where was Lobo? And what had been behind all the shooting and shouting he'd heard before passing out? The simple act of considering these matters increased the pain in his head and Brand lapsed into a shallow, restless sleep that was full of grey shadows and unseen dangers. He thought he heard voices again, far off and muted. He tried to identify them but drifted off into unconsciousness again.

A long time later he roused himself and found that the pain had lessened greatly. His detachment from reality had also faded and he was in full control of his senses now. He opened his eyes. This time the light was subdued, gentle. He realised it was early evening. He was lying on blankets, his body covered. Brand sensed he was being watched.

He turned to see who was there.

The brown, impassive face of Nante the Apache stared back at him. A ghost of a smile touched the old warrior's lips when he realised Brand had recognised him.

"Death has given up the struggle," Nante said.

"I'll take your word for it." Brand raised a hand to touch his battered face, feeling the thick stubble covering his jaw. "How long has it been?"

"This is the second night." Nante called to an Apache who squatted nearby. The Indian got up and padded across to the fire that blazed nearby. "There was little we could do for you, Brand. Although we cleaned your wounds the hurt was in your head. So we waited to see if you lived."

Brand watched the other Apache approach. There was a steaming mug in his hand. Brand sat up slowly, fighting against the nausea. The Apache passed him the mug. It was full of hot black coffee.

"This time I offer you coffee," Nante said.

"At least I'm alive to drink it."

"Brand, the woman is dead. Lobo killed her. We were too late to stop him."

Brand had been expecting something along those lines. If Elizabeth had been alive and well she would have come to him. Even so the blunt, sparse words spoken by the Apache bit deep. The memory of the scream he had heard during the final moments before blacking out came flooding back. Brand shuddered violently. She had died and he had been unable to prevent it happening. He recalled the night they had shared together; her last night alive, though neither of them had known it at the time.

He remembered something she had said.

"It never lasts does it!"

"Nante, did she die quickly?"

"What is quickly? She suffered — yet she spoke your name, Brand. Then she died."

Brand drained the mug of coffee. He stared around the campsite. He was lying just outside the cave. Gathered together by the fire were three Apaches, talking quietly among themselves. A number of horses milled around inside the corral. His own animal, and the one Elizabeth had ridden were among them.

"It was your horse that brought us here," Nante told him. "Though we had started south I began to have bad feelings about Lobo. My spirit shadow spoke to me and said Lobo would spill blood. I heeded his words and took three of my warriors. We came to help you, Brand. You are a friend of The People. We found tracks and followed them. Then we heard shooting. One of my warriors found your horse. We saw sign and found a dead man. And the sign led us up here to this place."

"Lobo?"

"He escaped us." This time even Nante was unable to keep the bitterness out of his voice. "He knows this place

166

better than we do. And our ponies were tired after the climb. Though we gave chase he avoided us and rode away."

Brand pushed the blankets aside and struggled to his feet. The world spun for a time. He stayed upright though, determined not to go down again. He didn't. It took time and it hurt, but he made it to the fire and helped himself to another mug of coffee. One of the Apaches offered him a hunk of hot, greasy meat. Brand wolfed it down. He wasn't sure what the meat was, though he had his own ideas. He was too hungry to worry.

"I know what is in your heart, Brand," Nante said as he joined Brand by the fire. "But you should rest longer."

Brand knew the Apache was right. He was still weak. On the other hand he couldn't allow Lobo too greater a lead. The renegade wouldn't be leaving an easy trail to follow and tracks didn't show for ever.

"Which way did he go, Nante?"

167

The old Apache sighed. "You would make a good Apache, Brand. Once I had your stubborn ways too."

"Nante, you've still got them. Now which way did he go?"

Nante beckoned one of the Apaches. "Che followed his trail the first day. Lobo rode down towards the Grande. He will not return to this place. And you wounded him, Brand. We talked and agree he will go west, then south. Beyond the Grande and into the badlands. Maybe Sonora."

The Apaches were making sense. The area they were describing would be ideal for Lobo's purpose. It was a lonely, sunbleached place. There was nothing but desert and rocky mountains. A part of New Mexico that jutted further south into Mexico than anywhere else along the border country. The Hatchet Mountains lay here, with Big Hatchet Peak rising to around 8,000 feet. It was barren country. A place where no one travelled unless they were forced to by circumstances. There were no regular trails. Or habitation. There was water if you knew where to find it. Years back the Apache raiding parties had used it when they made forays up out of Sonora and Chihuahua. Dead country, harsh, seared by the sun it might be, but to Lobo it would offer sanctuary. He would find himself a place to rest, to tend his wounds, knowing there would be little chance of being disturbed. If the need arose Lobo could lose himself for years in that barren corner of the territory. Biding his time. Letting nature heal old wounds and erase memories. There was always Mexico, still a haven, if he wanted to make use of it.

"I'll head out in the morning," Brand said, and Nante accepted his decision.

Brand took another chunk of the meat offered to him. Now that his initial hunger had been eased he took his time with this piece. He was able to taste the meat better this time. He was able to identify it too. Horsemeat. The Apache never wasted a thing. They

169

would take a near-dead horse and get another day's ride from it. When it finally did die on them they ate it. It was a pointer as to why the Apache had survived for so long in such a hostile environment. They became as one with the land. They learned not to fight it, but to exist alongside it, making use of it, wasting nothing.

As soon as he finished eating Brand decided to turn in. He accepted that Nante had been right. He did need more rest. But he also knew that he would not settle completely until he had settled with Lobo. He had a long, hard ride ahead of him. Through some rough country. But it was something he had to do.

"Nante, where is the woman?" he asked.

The Apache led him some way off. Elizabeth and Preacher Jude had been laid in a shallow depression and covered with rocks. Brand stared at the place for a time. He felt empty when he thought of Elizabeth. Her desire to help her half brother had cost her more than anyone should have needed to pay. Her offer of friendship had demanded a terrible price. Brand tried to recall her face. Her youthful beauty. But all he could remember was her final terrified scream.

"What did he do to her?" he asked.

Nante touched a brown finger to his stomach. He made a swift cutting motion, his finger moving up his chest. Then he repeated the gesture across his throat.

Brand's stomach knotted. Violent death was never pretty. It was brutal and sickening. He was well aware what could be done to the human body by an expertly wielded knife. He'd seen it happen and it was an ugly, mean way to die. To imagine Elizabeth dying in such a manner was akin to having a nightmare while awake. He was unable to resist the image of her beautiful body, lying naked beside him. Her soft flesh pale and warm. And then he saw the image change and those gentle curves were splashed with bright blood, the flesh ripped and violated. Life itself draining out of the ugly wounds.

He turned away from the grave and returned to the campsite. Nante followed, sensing Brand's despair.

"Ask and I will send warriors with you."

Brand shook his head. "No. He's mine, Nante. When I find him it'll be for everyone he's killed. White and Apache. But most of all it'll be for me."

He lay under his blanket. His body was ready for more rest. He didn't fight it. This time he wanted sleep to take him. If he hadn't he would have lain awake all night, seeing Elizabeth, hearing that damned scream, and knowing he'd been unable to help her when she needed him most — and that was the worst thing of all to have to accept!

15

A CHILL wind slanted in from the north. The early dawn was grey, the sky heavy with cloud. The wind snatched at the flames of the fire with greedy fingers, whipping the smoke away in ragged scraps.

Brand finished strapping on his saddle and gear. He had helped himself to what food he could find in the store Lobo had been forced to abandon and filled his canteen from the nearby pool. He had also taken the opportunity to replenish his ammunition supply. The remainder of the supplies, weapons and ammunition had been loaded onto the spare horse by Nante's warriors.

"This is for the times he has taken from The People," Nante said. He gestured at his warriors and they rode off across the basin.

"When you find him, Brand, kill him

well," Nante said.

"I aim to." Brand swung up into his own saddle. He was unable to stop himself from looking across at Elizabeth's grave.

"Only the living matter," Nante said, "The dead are no more than shadows that vanish with the dawn."

The old man was right. Brand had enough to occupy himself with. There was no point filling his mind with thoughts of Elizabeth's death. Once he got close to Lobo he would need to think clearly, his mind free of obscure images.

With Nante alongside Brand rode across the basin. He led out along the narrow passage until they emerged on the empty plateau. The three Apaches were already halfway down the long slope. Brand urged his horse over the crest and felt its muscles bunch as it took the strain. Dust floated up behind Brand and Nante, caught by the breeze and whipped away. Loose stones rattled dryly under the hooves of the passing horses. At the bottom of the slope he turned his horse along the defile. Finally they reached the spread of the valley.

By this time full light was on them. The greyness had vanished and the wind was dropping. The heat of the day began to make itself known to them.

The night's rest had done Brand some good. He found he could easily bear the headache that still lingered. Food in his stomach had quelled the earlier sickness. Though his body was stiff and awkward in the saddle he persevered.

The valley fell behind them and they came out on the high slope of the mountain. It was here that they parted company.

"I will listen for how it goes with you, Brand," Nante said.

Brand nodded. He wondered if he would ever see the old warrior again. The time of the Apache was short. They would fight until the last possible moment, and though it would be a hard thing to do Brand was sure that the great leaders of the tribes would make their peace. When they did a long and proud reign would end, and a unique race of fighting men would be disarmed and put out to grass.

"Watch out for Army patrols near the border," Brand said. "Make new trails for your people, Nante."

He turned his horse west and pushed on. The young Apache named Che had found Lobo's trail earlier and though it was faint, Brand was able to follow it. The renegade had a good lead, but he was wounded and he had quit his hideout without supplies. There were a few small outfits along the banks of the Rio Grande, and it was possible that Lobo might choose one of these isolated places to raid. He would be looking for food and ammunition, maybe even medical supplies.

He rode steadily, resisting the urge to push his horse. He had a long way to go so there was no point tiring the animal too soon. The high peaks slipped away behind him as he rode down out of the high country, through the treeline. He kept moving after dark and it was close to midnight when he made camp. He saw to his horse after tethering it close to the edge of a shallow, cold stream with thin grass sprouting along its edge. Building a small fire he heated water for coffee then warmed some beans and ate them with some beef jerky. He drank three mugs of hot, black coffee before turning in. He slept until dawn was already lighting the sky.

Around midmorning he found himself on a ridge looking down at the ribbon of water known as the Rio Grande. Nante's thoughts were proving correct. The tracks Brand had been following west were now starting to ease to the south. Once beyond the river those tracks would curve harder south, heading for the foothills of the Hatchet Range. Brand rode down off the ridge and pushed on towards the river, his way taking him across the Mesilla Valley. He made the river crossing as darkness fell and camped on the west bank of the Grande.

He was saddled and riding again before dawn. As the day brightened around him he found he could make out the hazy peaks of the Hatchets far ahead.

Lobo's tracks turned sharp south. The renegade was staying close to the river. Brand wondered why. He figured there might be a couple of reasons. The first seemed obvious — water — but Lobo knew the land well enough not to have to depend on the river for his supply. The second reason made more sense. Lobo *did* need food and ammunition. So he would be looking for some lonely outfit. A place where he could tend his wound and pick up the supplies he needed.

Brand came on the place just before noon. It was a small spread. A low adobe house and a small corral. A shallow feeder stream ran by the house, emptying into the Grande less than a half mile away. A hot breeze was keening across the dry, sunbaked landscape as Brand rode in and surveyed the ugly scene of desolation spread out before him. This tiny place, with its stark house had been the beginning of a family's dream — now it had become their nightmare.

A man's body lay half submerged in the creek. He lay on his back, sightless eyes staring up into the sun. He had been shot three times in the chest. The wounds were big and ugly; the kind of wound caused by an expanding bullet; the kind Lobo used. Thick masses of black flies crawled in and around the wounds. Brand rode through the creek and on towards the house. He could see objects scattered on the yard. Smashed furniture and crockery. Torn clothing. Books ripped to shreds in a frenzy of needless violence. In the corral were two dead horses. The carcases were being devoured by buzzards. The ugly birds were screeching at each other, greedy to the last despite their being ample meat for them all. Closer to the house Brand saw another body. Another man, younger than the one in the water. Brand dismounted and took his rifle as he walked to the house. Passing the body he saw that the man was naked to the waist, his torso slashed open from throat to stomach. Brand paused by the body and couldn't help wondering if this was how Elizabeth had looked.

He halted at the open door to the house. The smell that reached him from the interior was heavy and sickly-sweet. It was a smell he knew only too well. There was only one room. It had been ransacked, torn apart. Worse though were the great splashes of blood that marked walls and floor. he found two more bodies — both women. They were almost naked, their clothing having been shredded from their bodies. One was around forty, the other no more than eighteen. Brand felt nausea rise up in his throat as he looked at them. They had been crudely butchered, their flesh hacked and slashed with cruel deliberation.

The sight brought dark memories flooding into Brand's tired mind. The remembrance of someone else — another pretty girl who had died in such a way. Brand had been slowly erasing that particular image. The sight of his own wife, lying dead and silent, the victim of a brutal, vengeful man who had cut her to pieces. The killer had still been there when Brand had come home. And Brand, in a moment of madness, had fought with the man and put him under his own knife before he had died. It had been vengeance pure and simple, but it had not brought back Brand's wife or eased his pain.

He went outside, leaning against the house wall as revulsion rose in his throat. He stayed where he was until the feeling passed. When he returned to his horse there was a sheen of cold sweat on his ashen face. He gathered the reins and climbed into the saddle. Leaning against the saddlehorn he stared out across the land, his gaze fixed on the distant mountains. Somewhere ahead of him was Lobo, maybe even knowing he was being followed. It was possible that what Brand had found here was a silent warning. A threat to make him aware of what he was letting himself in for. If it was, it had backfired, because it only made Brand more determined to stay on Lobo's trail.

The tracks leading away from the spread were still clear. They were moving directly southwest. Lobo was making straight for the Hatchets. He had got what he wanted from the homestead. Now he would be going to ground, hoping to lose himself once he reached the mountain range.

Brand increased his pace now. He pushed his horse as fast as he dared. The terrain was dun coloured, slightly undulating. A mix of desert and rockbeds. It was desolate, burned out country. There were dusty, silent canyons, places that rarely echoed to the sound of a human voice. In the far distance, where the foothills of the Hatchet Range rose out of the flagrant, the dun colouring merged with the yellow, brown and pinks of the exposed rock strata. Higher up the slopes became hazy blue, soft against the coppery sky. There was little vegetation in evidence. Some cholla. A little ironwood and cat's claw, with its hooked thorns and yellow blossoms. It was a primitive landscape, cruel by nature and as such it accepted violence as a natural extension of itself.

Brand rode without pause, through the crippling heat of the afternoon and into the night. The moon rose and bathed the land in a cold, ghostly light. Brand stopped once, in the early hours of the morning, to rest his horse while he chewed on a strip of jerky. He shared his water with his horse, making a mental note to watch out for a chance of refilling his canteen. Then he remounted, draping his blanket across his shoulders to keep out some of the chill that came along with the night wind. That same wind grew warm, then hot as daylight brightened the landscape around him. It burned his skin and threw sand in his face. He could hear it moaning softly as he rode by desolate canyons, where the soft, fine sand, drifting for endless years, had formed fantastic shapes against the crumbling cliffs.

The hours passed. Brand showed no outer signs of exhaustion. There would be time for sleep when his trail reached its end. Now he had too much on his mind. He was closing on the foothills, and this was the time when he could expect trouble to show itself. He held his rifle across his saddle now, his finger close to the trigger. Brand's hat was pulled low across his face to shield his eyes from the glare of the sun.

He drew rein. For a long time he studied the tracks in the sand. They rose up a long, sunbaked slope before him. He eased from the saddle. Taking the reins in his left hand he led his horse up the slope. Reaching the top he stood and scanned the landscape, searching the crumbling, broken slopes that rose in irregular steps. There was an unearthly silence to this terrain. It was evidence of a land with little growing on it. Virtually no plants. Utterly devoid of human presence. The land held its silence because it sustained no life.

Brand didn't move on for a long time. Not until he was entirely satisfied. He carried on walking, grateful to be able to stretch his legs. He had been in the saddle for too long a time. He felt dirty and unshaven. His clothes were thick with caked dust and stale with sweat. It streaked his burned, battered face. The relentless sun hammered down on him. Even the ground underfoot was hot, the shifting sand burning through the soles of his boots.

Noon of another day. He knew he had to be close now. He had made good time travelling through the night. He squinted up at the rearing rock canyons and ravines that stretched before him. Somewhere within that maze of rock and sand was Lobo. Maybe the renegade had him in his sights even now. Brand doubted it. He knew that if Lobo got even half a chance at hitting Brand he'd take it.

He picked his way along a dried out watercourse strewn with tumbled rocks. The heat of the sun bounced off the hard ground and slapped back against him with a physical force. Brand pushed his way through a tangle of dead ironwood. As he pulled his horse clear a lizard darted out from beneath a rock. It ran in front of his horse, causing it to jerk back, eyes rolling. As Brand yanked down on the reins the animal gave a shrill whinny of protest.

And from somewhere up the slope ahead came an answering call from another horse. The sound touched Brand's ears, and he reacted fast. Hauling in the slack reins he dragged his horse, still protesting, close in to the overhanging bank of the long dead river.

There was quick movement ahead. Stones rattled down the slope. The whiplash crack of a rifle shattered the silence with deafening clarity. The bullet slammed off the eroded stone edging the bank. It howled off into the sky, the clattering echo rippling outwards.

Brand levered a round into the Winchester's breech. He looped the horse's reins around an exposed root. *Now's the time*, he thought. Lobo had made the first move. Instead of waiting he had taken a quick shot, wasting a bullet and exposing his position. Not that Brand cared. He wanted his man and he wasn't going to worry over the way it had come about.

He eased away from where he had tethered the horse, moving yards from his original position. Only then did he show himself above the bank. It was so he could check the way ahead, trying to pinpoint Lobo's exact position.

As Brand cleared the rim of the bank he saw movement on the rocky slope above him. He spotted a dark face, framed by long hair, the bright sun glinting on the brass cases of the bullets in the bandolier around Lobo's neck. Without a pause Brand swung the Winchester to his shoulder. He caught the moving figure in his sights, held, led the figure for an instant. He touched the trigger, the rifle cracking loudly. Brand saw Lobo leap back, a splash of red appearing on his left shoulder. He knew he had made a good shot. Almost too late he saw the flash of sunlight on a rifle barrel as Lobo ranged in. The half-breed fired. The bullet struck rock inches away, driving stone chips into Brand's face. He felt the sting as they gouged his flesh, felt the warm trickle of blood down his cheek. He pulled back from the bank, moving on, and when he looked out again Lobo had already changed *his* position. Brand caught a glimpse of his running figure heading for higher ground. He raised the rifle and snapped off hasty shots, seeing the bullets raise dirt around Lobo's legs moments before the renegade rolled out of sight behind a crumbling shelf of rock.

Brand climbed over the rim of the bank and made for the slope. He wasn't about to let Lobo vanish into the canyons ahead. There were too many good places where a man could hide and even lay an ambush. Brand wanted to keep Lobo out in the open as much as possible. Keep him on the move. Under pressure. He did not want to have to search for Lobo within the maze of vaulted, tortuous rocks.

He passed the spot where Lobo had stood. The renegade's pony stood patiently waiting. Brand moved on up the slope, treading carefully as he crossed a loose patch of ground. In the moment he reached the top of the slope he caught a glimpse of movement off to the right. He dropped, hugging his rifle to him as he rolled across the rocky earth. He heard the crash of a rifle, felt the bullets whack the ground close by. There was a pause, followed by more shots. Brand felt a bullet burn across his back. He ignored the stinging sensation. Gathering his legs under him he pushed to his feet. As he moved he searched for Lobo.

He almost missed the half-breed when he did show.

Brand was level with a rising hump of smooth rock. He heard a faint whisper of sound. As his head came round he caught a glimpse of a taut, angry face, eyes wild with hate. Then a lunging figure flew through the air at him. Lobo smashed against Brand and they hit the ground locked together, twisting and turning, each seeking an advantage over the other. They came to rest against a squat boulder. For a moment they remained bound together, then Brand twisted free and rolled away. He pushed to his feet. Lobo was equally as swift. He arched up off the ground, snatching his knife free. Brand saw the gleaming blade and pushed back. He began to swing up the Winchester, but Lobo lunged forward and the tip of the knife blade sliced through Brand's shirt and gouged the flesh beneath. He knew he wasn't going to get the rifle in line for a shot as Lobo came in again, the pale blade cutting the air. Brand lashed out with the heavy rifle, the butt cracking down on Lobo's knife hand. The knife spun from numbed fingers. Lobo kicked out, driving his foot into Brand's ribs. The blow had enough force behind it to slam Brand back against a low rock. Lying there Brand saw Lobo almost on him. The renegade sledged a hard fist across the side of Brand's neck, spilling him to the ground. Brand pulled his aching body away from Lobo's slashing foot as the half-breed closed in. He had almost got clear when something solid halted further retreat. He had come to rest against a heavy boulder. As Brand drew his legs under him, starting to push erect, Lobo's foot caught him across the mouth. The blow snapped his head back, blood bursting from split lips. The force of the blow slammed his head into the rock behind him, pain exploding in his skull. The agony was intense, like the pain he had felt back at Lobo's hideout. Brand realised that if he didn't get up now he never would. He arched his body away from the boulder, swinging the Winchester at Lobo's legs. He felt the rifle connect with a solid impact. Lobo grunted. Brand struck again. Lobo fell back. On his feet Brand hauled the rifle round and as it levelled he snapped off a shot. The bullet hit Lobo in the left side, and this time it went in deep. Lobo roared in agony, turning away, seeking a way of escape.

Fighting back the pain in his skull Brand paused to lever another round into the Winchester's breech. His fingers refused to work as fast as they might. He was still groggy from the blow to his head. Finally, after

what seemed an eternity, Brand closed
the lever. He raised his head, lifting
the rifle.

He was alone.

Lobo had gone!

16

LOBO ran.

He ran because he was hurt. Badly hurt and he needed somewhere to rest, time to look to his wounds. His shoulder, though painful, was the less serious. The second bullet fired by the man named Brand had lodged deep in his body, and though it had not touched a vital organ it had opened a wound that was bleeding steadily. His body burned with pain too. A searing, constant pain that raged inside. He could not fight while the pain lasted, so he had turned away, which was against his nature. Lobo might have been fanatical in his pursuit of vengeance, but he was not suicidal. There was no point in carrying on while he was at a disadvantage. That was foolishness. So he retreated, seeking a place to hide. So he could mend his damaged body and regain his strength.

Things were going against him. The reversal had forced him to abandon his hideout in the San Andres and to come here to the Hatchet badlands. The discovery of his previous hideout had rendered it useless. He could never return to it. Lobo regretted that. But it was not essential. He could always find himself another retreat. Just as secret. That was for the future. First he had to recover from the wounds inflicted by the man name Brand. Lobo felt anger because he had failed to kill Brand. The man was more than a professional. He was a born killer. A natural hunter. A man close to Lobo in his way of life. Already they had come close to killing each other. Lobo knew his man now, so he was aware that for as long as he carried breath in his body Brand would keep coming after his quarry. It would not end until one of them was dead.

He thrust forward through a thorny thicket, ignoring the pain of the barbs that clawed at his flesh. He had one object in mind. To get away from Brand. To find a good place to hide.

He bitterly regretted having to abandon his pony. In his pack there was food and medicine from the spread he had raided. Disposing of the four people had been easy, especially the women. He had kept them alive until he had used them to satisfy his lust, and had killed them afterwards with casual ease. Now his supplies were far behind him, even his water. He would find more. He knew the country well. Had the locations of natural springs and water sources etched on his mind. He even knew where he could find food and vegetation he could use to make medicines. He had been forced into situations like this before. Having to exist off the land, pursued by his enemies. And he had survived every time. He would do it again, despite being hurt. Perhaps because he *was* hurt. At times like these he lived up to his name. Lobo. The wolf. At his best when he was cornered. Forced to fight to live.

But first he would withdraw. The bullet he carried would bring him pain and the pain would make him weak. Before that happened he had to find his refuge. Somewhere that would provide protection. Lobo knew Brand was still behind him. Still searching. Despite his need for rest Lobo might yet have to face his adversary. If that happened Lobo would kill him. If he could avoid a fight now he would do so, resting and recovering. So the priority was a place to hide. If he collapsed out in the open Brand would find him and kill him. He knew enough about the man to accept that Brand would destroy him without hesitation. Brand would never forget that Lobo had killed the girl who called herself Elizabeth Henty. She had been a fool. Half-sister or not, she had been dead the moment she set foot in the San Andres. Lobo had learned long ago not to allow sentiment to affect his judgement. Emotions ruled many mens' hearts, and in times of danger a man who let himself be weakened by those emotions was half defeated before he went into conflict. Lobo had no ties. No loyalties to cloud his judgement. He depended upon no one but himself, and that way there could be no mistakes save his own. No risk to survival because of someone else. He existed for himself alone. Not for his dead Apache mother, or his dead white father; he had disowned both many years ago, hating them for the legacy they had bestowed on him. Half-breed! For that he could never forgive them. If circumstances had made it possible he would have killed them himself.

In the shadow of a massive boulder he rested. His body pulsed with the pain of his wounds. The shoulder had stopped bleeding. But the wound in his side still wept. His constant running had only increased the flow. But he could not rest properly until he found some place to hide himself from the eyes of the world. He scanned the slopes and ridges around him, searching the shadowed places in the tangled brush. The man named Brand was somewhere close by. There was no doubt in the renegade's mind. Brand would follow until one or both of them died. He was a worthy opponent. Lobo had learned a grudging respect for the man as an enemy. Brand was a survivor — and that was the secret. To survive whatever the cost, whatever the odds. To stay alive and carry on the fight. It was the code by which Lobo lived, and it had served him well all these years. It would serve him in the future.

Lobo's vigilance gained him nothing. There was no sound or sight of Brand. Yet Lobo knew as night followed day that Brand was out there. He would show himself when the time was right. And this time someone would die.

When he was rested Lobo slipped away from his sheltering boulder and moved on. He found a narrow canyon that cut its dusty way into the rock. He ran to the entrance, his passing a mere whisper of sound. Hot sand sifted beneath his feet. Faint spirals of dust hung in the air after he had gone.

It was even hotter in the canyon. The trapped air held the heat like a muffling blanket. Lobo felt it wrap around him. The sunlight bounced back off the rock, hurting his eyes. Under normal circumstances such things never bothered him, but in his weakened state his resistance had been reduced. He moved his dry lips, feeling the parched skin crack and bleed. He needed water. Pausing he gazed around the canyon. There would be water somewhere. It was simply a case of finding it. Not here in the main canyon, but in one of the smaller side-canyons. It was often in these isolated pockets that a man could find water, even grass and shade. There might even be food. The wildlife of the area would know of these secret water holes. A patient man might find all he needed in one of these places.

It took him over two hours, but he finally located a likely side-canyon. It was narrow, full of twists and turns. Lobo followed it for more than a half-mile, and he was beginning to believe he had made a mistake. Then he saw patches of greenery and soon after a small spring bubbling out of a fissure. The water collected in a shallow pan, the overspill creating a narrow stream that meandered across the canyon floor. Lobo knelt at the spring to drink, taking care not to swallow too much. After drinking he splashed water over his face, opening his shirt to wet his body. The cool water felt good against his dry, sunburned flesh.

Crouching by the spring he debated his next move. He had water. Now he needed a place to hide, close by yet well concealed. He searched the immediate area, locating a low cave that cut its way into the canyon wall. The entrance was narrow, low to the ground, with a lip just inside. The cave floor dropped away just beyond the lip. It provided protection that was easy to defend from inside. A mass of cat's

201

claw concealed part of the entrance. Lobo crawled inside to look round. It would do for his needs, he decided. He came outside again. From deep inside the cat's claw, where the break would not be noticed, he snapped off a length of the bush. He retraced his steps back along the canyon, then returned once again to the cave, wiping away his tracks as he did so. He eased into the cave, having erased all his footprints, even those around the spring.

Now all he could do was rest and wait. It was against his nature to allow weakness to rule his actions, but for once he had no choice. Now he was inactive he could feel the overwhelming nausea dulling his senses. The bullet inside him was still affecting him. He knew it had to come out soon, before it poisoned his whole body. He would do that himself, but first he needed to rest. Later he could build a fire and heat the blade of his knife . . .

Lobo let his body relax. He tried to detach himself from the pain, focussing his attention on the sunbright canyon. When Brand did come it would be along there. Lobo eased his Colt from its holster, drawing back the hammer. He laid the gun where he could easily reach it.

Brand would have to come very close before he spotted the cave. At close range it would only take one shot — one well-placed bullet — and it would be all be over. Lobo smiled to himself. A cold and merciless smile.

The wolf was not dead yet!

17

BRAND lost the trail for a time. It made him angry because he was following a wounded man who had made attempt to cover his tracks. Here and there he found dark bloodstains. He wasn't sure just how badly Lobo was hurt, but he had put two bullets in the half-breed and they had to count for something. On the other hand Lobo was not like ordinary men. He possessed a strength of will that would drag him to Hell and back before he even thought about quitting. Brand figured that Lobo would be looking for somewhere to hole up. A place where he could rest and regain some of the strength he had already lost. He had nothing with him in the way of supplies. His only weapons were his handgun and his knife. Lobo was in a desperate position. He would be feeling cornered. And like a wild animal he would put his back to the wall and fight.

Tiring of casting about aimlessly Brand reined in and climbed down out of the saddle. His head still ached, the sun was scorching him and he was dry. He reached for his canteen and took a swallow of lukewarm water. Leading his horse he moved on. Still searching. Minutes later he spotted a faint footprint in the dust. Brand turned towards it. Ahead he picked out more tracks. They were still heading up into the mountains. Lobo was seeking the high ground, searching for some lofty, desolate place to hide.

He came to the canyon an hour later. Something about the place told him this was where Lobo would go. When he reached the canyon mouth he saw that the tracks went in. Taking out his Colt Brand went into the canyon, feeling the reflected heat strike him. He walked the dusty, twisting canyon floor, studying Lobo's tracks and trying to place himself in the half-breed's mind. Imagining what Lobo was thinking.

The answer came with startling clarity.

Water!

That would Lobo's prime need.

The renegade had nothing. He would need to find a place where there was water to drink and clean his wounds. And usually where there was water came other things. To provide food. There was also a need for somewhere for Lobo to hide.

He spotted the side-canyon and the tracks leading into it. Securing his horse Brand stepped into the narrow canyon. He stood for a time, not wanting to move ahead until he had the feel of the place. It was well suited to Lobo's needs. There were countless places for a man to hide. The sudden bends and twists put the odds in favour of anyone defending the place. Brand walked on, aware that an attack could come at any time.

He was well into the canyon when

the tracks he was following abruptly vanished. Brand realised he was getting close now. The only way those tracks could stop so completely was because they had been deliberately wiped away.

Brand pressed in close to the side of the canyon, searching the way ahead. At first glance there didn't appear to be anything different about this section. Just sand and rock. Motionless. Silent.

He kept on going. The sand on the canyon floor was unmarked, save for a faint pattern of soft swirls breaking the surface. Brand had seen enough tracks wiped away with a length of leafy foliage to recognise the signs. He was in the right place. No doubt about it now.

Some time later his eye was caught by a small patch of green. Grass! Brand looked again and saw the sparkle of water bubbling out of the rock. A spring. That would be what Lobo would have been searching for. Brand eyed the canyon sides. They were far too steep to allow any climbing. So where was Lobo?

Brand started to turn away, when he spotted a clump of cat's claw growing against the base of the canyon wall. Something about it caught his attention. He felt certain he had seen a sliver of brightness behind the dusty foliage. It had been a brief flicker, over as fast as it had occurred, but there had been enough to catch his eye. He continued his turn, hoping he hadn't made his observation noticeable. He wanted to see more, if there was something to see. Because under normal circumstances there shouldn't have been anything to glitter in a desolate place like this. To Brand the flash of brightness brought to mind the brass cartridge cases filling the loops in Lobo's bandolier.

He walked on, the Colt at his side. His finger lay against the trigger, thumb resting lightly on the hammer. Brand allowed his gaze to wander, attempting to give the impression he was still looking. If he'd been correct he wanted to draw Lobo into making a move that might expose him.

Nothing happened. Brand felt a trickle of sweat course down his back. It was possible he'd been wrong. But he had learned long ago to act on impulse. Going with his instincts. Right or wrong he made his choices — and lived with them.

He kept moving. The mass of cat's claw lay only yards ahead and to his left. Brand was in the open. He couldn't have offered a better target.

Out of the corner of his eye he caught the same flicker of reflected light. It lasted no more than a second, vanished, then reappeared. This time it moved, seeming to push forward through the foliage.

Brand threw himself to the right, hearing the blast of a gunshot. As he hit the ground, turning his body, he felt the closeness of the passing bullet. He was lying flat then, thrusting his Colt towards the place where the shot had come from. He triggered two quick shots then altered his position, the Colt cocked and ready for firing again. As he came to rest he saw the lithe form of Lobo sliding easily out of a narrow gap at the base of the canyon wall. The renegade had his own gun in his hand and it swept round to line up on Brand, spitting flame and smoke in a crash of sound. The bullet clipped the top of Brand's left shoulder, burning the flesh. He ignored the pain, coming up on one knee, his Colt tracking in on the renegade as Lobo straightened up. Brand's shot took him in the left hip, slamming him back against the canyon wall, blood flying in a scarlet spray. Lobo bared his teeth in a snarl of defiance, eyes wild with fury. He steadied himself against the rock, lifting his heavy Colt. Brand fired first, his Colt held two-handed. He put all three remaining .45 calibre bullets into Lobo's chest. The impact kicked Lobo back. His mouth opened in a soundless scream of agony. He hung against the canyon wall, his shirt blossoming red. And then he fell face down, his spilled blood being quickly swallowed by the dry, thirsty sand.

Brand walked to where the renegade lay. He picked up Lobo's revolver and tucked it under his belt. He knelt beside the body and rolled it over. He could relax now. The half-breed renegade called Lobo was dead.

"I hope you fry in hell, you son of a bitch," he said softly, and meant every word. He was thinking about Elizabeth, who had died alone and helpless on a desolate mountain slope. And about all the others who had suffered at the hands of the embittered man who had been born Matthew Henty.

He stood up, turning away and made his way back along the canyon to find his horse. Then he had to find Lobo's pony so he could cart Lobo's body back to Fort Kellerman. There was a job he had to do before he headed for the Army post. There were four people who needed a decent burial. He was going to ride back to that little spread near the Rio Grande and see to that first. Then he would take Lobo's body to Kellerman and let Alex Mundy officially close the book on the renegade.

And then? He figured a slow return to Washington. Take a break for some rest before McCord grabbed him for something else.

He was wrong. McCord was waiting for him at Kellerman. He barely had time to say hello to Mundy before Frank McCord was heading him for the nearest rail depot and a train to Washington. Brand had time for a bath and shave at Kellerman made a visit to the post doctor to have his wounds cleaned and bandaged, and then he was on his way. Ill at ease in his crumpled suit and still tense from the long trip back to Kellerman, Brand hunched in the corner of the private compartment and tried to pay attention to what McCord was saying.

"You can write your report while you rest up," he said.

"I get to rest?"

"Don't take too long," McCord went on. "You only have a few days."

"Days? Hell, McCord, I figured at least a week."

"No chance," McCord said, obviously enjoying himself. "As soon as possible I want you ready for your next assignment."

"Damnit, McCord, what's happened to all your other operatives? They up and quit on you?"

McCord allowed himself a frosty smile. "Nobody ever quits on me, Brand. I like to keep my people."

"So why am I so popular?"

"Because you are the only man who can tackle this particular assignment." McCord leaned forward. "Remember when you'd been with the US Marshal office for a year? You were on assignment in Galveston. The case involved a series of murders of prominent businessmen. It turned out they were the work of a hired killer. You broke the case but the assassin got away."

"I remember."

"The killer was a man who had never been identified. No one had ever seen him face to face. You did, Brand. You saw his face. Would you know him again?"

Brand nodded. "I'd know him."

"Good. That's why you and this assignment go together."

McCord leaned back in his seat and stared out of the window, gathering his thoughts.

"In a week a British Lord will arrive in Washington. He's a member of the British Government, and because of his involvement with extensive investments here, he's a guest of the United States Government. While he's in the country he intends to do a lot of travelling. Mainly he will be based in Montana. He'll be attending the Stockgrowers Convention up in Miles City, and afterwards he'll go further north. You will be with him, Brand, from the moment he sets foot outside his hotel in Washington."

"There a good reason?"

"Our information has it that while he's here someone is going to try to kill him. The reason you are on the assignment is that our information states that the man being paid to do the killing is the assassin known as Raven. The man you almost caught. The man you can identify by sight."

Brand closed his eyes and decided to catch some sleep. He figured he might as well get as much as he could during the trip. Once he was back in Washington it didn't look as if he would get the opportunity. McCord and his new assignment would see to that.

THE END

FIGHTING RAMROD
Charles N. Heckelmann

Most men would have cut their losses, but Frazer counted the bullets in his guns and said he'd soak the range in blood before he'd give up another inch of what was his.

LONE GUN
Eric Allen

Smoke Blackbird had been away too long. The Lequires had seized the Blackbird farm, forcing the Indians and settlers off, and no one seemed willing to fight! He had to fight alone.

THE THIRD RIDER
Barry Cord

Mel Rawlins wasn't going to let anything stand in his way. His father was murdered, his two brothers gone. Now Mel rode for vengeance.

ARIZONA DRIFTERS
W. C. Tuttle

When drifting Dutton and Lonnie Steelman decide to become partners they find that they have a common enemy in the formidable Thurston brothers.

TOMBSTONE
Matt Braun

Wells Fargo paid Luke Starbuck to outgun the silver-thieving stagecoach gang at Tombstone. Before long Luke can see the only thing bearing fruit in this eldorado will be the gallows tree.

HIGH BORDER RIDERS
Lee Floren

Buckshot McKee and Tortilla Joe cut the trail of a border tough who was running Mexican beef into Texas. They stopped the smuggler in his tracks.